THE DERRY SPY

BY

FRANK NASH

Copyright © 2021 by FRANK NASH
All rights reserved
ISBN:

Special thanks to Daniel Constantinou, who told me to, "Just get out there and write."

The Organisations Explained

<u>The A14 Intelligence Company</u> also known as "The Det" were an elite detachment of army personnel established during the Troubles. Trained in armed and unarmed combat, advanced driving, surveillance, firearms and photography. They received very little publicity or plaudits, but were a vital force to The British Army in Northern Ireland.

<u>Ulster Volunteer Force (UVF)</u> Protestant terrorist group that emerged in 1966. It's first leader was an ex British Army soldier. Declared a ceasefire in 1994 and officially ended its campaign in 2007.

<u>Ulster Defence Association.</u> (UDA) Protestant terrorist group formed in 1971 as an umbrella group for various loyalist groups and undertook an armed campaign for 24 years.

<u>Irish Republican Army (IRA)</u> Catholic terrorist group originally formed in 1917 to fight against the British for Irish Independence. The subsequent Catholic paramilitary organisation seeking a united Ireland were officially known as The Provisional IRA but were still simply called the IRA.

<u>Royal Ulster Constabulary (RUC)</u> The Northern Ireland Police Force.

Londonderry is always referred to as Derry by the Catholic population.

This book is based on real events and individuals, but in the interests of privacy the majority of names have been changed.

In simple terms, a loyalist is someone who does not want a united Ireland and wishes to stay part of The United Kingdom. A republican is someone who would like to see a united Ireland that governs itself.

Table of Contents

Prologue ix
CHAPTER ONE Happy Christmas, 1989 1
CHAPTER TWO The Windmills of your Mind,
    January 1989 9
CHAPTER THREE Queen and Country 1989 22
CHAPTER FOUR A Quiet Life in the
    Country March 1999 33
CHAPTER FIVE Just a cup of coffee,
    March 1989 36
CHAPTER SIX The Sound of Music, 1999 51
CHAPTER SEVEN Home, March 1999 56
CHAPTER EIGHT Rise and Shine,
    March 1999 72
CHAPTER NINE Sister Mary Comes to Me,
    March 1999 84
CHAPTER TEN Welcome to Dublin,
    March 1999 95
CHAPTER ELEVEN Lost in France April 1999 114
CHAPTER TWELVE Breaking Glass 122
CHAPTER THIRTEEN Paperback writer,
    April 1999 135

CHAPTER FOURTEEN Mcloed Road 153
CHAPTER FIFTEEN Danny Boy 171
CHAPTER SIXTEEN The Offertory,
    April 1999 188
CHAPTER SEVENTEEN A very good Friday,
    October 1999 198
CHAPTER EIGHTEEN 374 Yards,
    November 1999 205
CHAPTER NINETEEN It's been fun.
    October 1999 211
CHAPTER TWENTY Fore! November 2000 223
CHAPTER TWENTY-ONE Two of Us 228

Prologue

By 1921 the demand for self-rule in Ireland was gaining pace. The British solution, was to give the mainly Catholic counties in the south their wishes, but the dominant Protestant population in the counties in the north, stayed under British rule and became known as Northern Ireland.

Things remained the same for forty years, until the growing Catholic population wanted more and because of this, the civil rights movement began to grow.

In areas such as Londonderry, the majority were being governed by the minority.

Up until the mid-1960's, there had been little violence, until one night in 1966, after finishing their shift in a pub called The Malvern Arms, four Catholic lads went late night drinking in a Protestant bar. They had no reason to feel unsafe, however, four-gun men fired at them as they left the bar and Peter Ward aged 18 was shot dead. The Protestant Ulster Defence Force claimed responsibility. He was one of three Catholics killed that month.

Within three years, rioting reached new levels and had by then exhausted the RUC so, the Northern Irish Government now led by Prime Minster James Chichester Clarke, asked the British Government to deploy the army to restore order.

Without doubt, the army stopped a civil war, but as reforms were rolled out, Protestant loyalists attacked the army. The most violent confrontation being the Battle of Shankill Road where the two sides, both carrying the Union Jack, fought each other. On the other side of the divide, the Catholic population and the army were having a "honeymoon" period, with soldiers receiving tea and biscuits whilst on patrol.

At this point in time, Catholic Republican activists saw an opportunity. In Athlone in December 1969, the Provisional IRA was formed. It had three principles, to defend Catholic areas, take retaliatory action and all-out war. In April 1970, the tea and biscuits period ended and the Royal Scots Guards, seen by The Catholics as Protestant soldiers were attacked by the IRA and the general Catholic community.

Conflict was truly underway and two years later, the British Army made what would be its biggest mistake in the entirety of the troubles. During a protest march by the

Prologue

Northern Ireland Civil Rights Association against internment, British paratrooper's shot 26 civilians, killing fourteen. This incident became known as Bloody Sunday.

What followed was another 25 years of conflict and over 3000 deaths until secret talks took place between John Hume, the moderate SDLP leader and Gerry Adams, (the leader of Sinn Fein, the political wing of the IRA). Hume convinced Adams to compromise with the UK and Southern Irish government. (Ironically the IRA at one time considered assassinating Hume).

In 1997 talks headed by U.S. Senator George Mitchell began. All sides had to be committed to non-violence for a place at the table. The following year all sides signed The Good Friday Agreement, apart from Ian Paisley's Protestant Democratic Unionist Party. 71% of voters from both sides of the Irish border voted in favour of it. Part of the agreement was the release of paramilitary prisoners. Paisley eventually compromised and became first minister alongside ex IRA bomber, Martin McGuiness. (Ironically, they became known as the Chuckle Brothers, such was their rapport) As for the paramilitaries on both sides, these included many prisoners convicted of maiming and murder, but were now free men and women. Some chose to turn their back on violence, others wanted revenge.

CHAPTER ONE

Happy Christmas, 1989

It's Christmas Eve 1989 and the Londonderry shops, despite the troubles, are full of shoppers and decorations. Most of The Northern Irish population hoped for a killing free Christmas. Lately, Protestant loyalists, had become the provinces most prolific killers. The most violent were the "Shanklin Butchers," who were randomly snatching Catholics off the street at night, to torture and kill. Relatives of suspected IRA members were being targeted which was sending shock waves throughout the Catholic community.

Across town, Captain Michael Quinn, thirty-four years old, six foot one, is standing in the doorway of a closed side door of the Northern Bank, an imposing building opposite Magazine Gate, one of the four entrances to the walled city. To a passer-by he could easily be a husband waiting for his wife to finish work, whilst sheltering from the snow, which was blowing in across from the River Foyle. He could hear the Christmas music being played in one of the near-by shops. His cigarette glowed in the darkened entrance. He moved from side to side, stamping his cold feet on the granite floor. The bell rang from the clock tower, it was six o'clock. Quinn was watching the door of the pub which the landlord had just opened. He stubbed out the cigarette and walked down the three steps onto the snow that had been falling heavily for around two hours.

Hands in pockets, his feet crunched on the fallen snow. As he crossed the road, he quickly leapt onto the pavement as a passing car with two young lads in it, beeped. He could hear their laughter through the open car window. He entered through the outside cage* of the Gainsborough Bar, which no one was manning yet.

The pub was a mixed bar, where both Protestants and Catholics drank. However, this fact, hadn't prevented it from being bombed back in 1977. There was a very sad looking Christmas tree, just inside the main door, decorated half-heartedly with some old Christmas lights blinking over tired tinsel. Quinn positioned himself on one of the empty stools up at the bar, watching the door.

"What'll you be having?" said the barman, wiping the bar area in front of Quinn, moving an ash tray and placing a paper coaster down.

Happy Christmas, 1989

"Glass of Smithwick's please." Said Quinn, in his perfected Dublin accent.

The barman slowly filled a glass.

"Haven't seen you in here before. You up from Dublin?"

"Aye, delivering a car."

He took a fresh pack of Benson and Hedges cigarettes from his coat pocket and ran his thumb nail along the cellophane strip. He lit a cigarette and leant his forearms on the edge of the bar lost in his thoughts.

Two nights before, there'd been a raid on a house in the Bogside area, not far from where he was sitting. The commander of the raid, Captain Jacob Candy had lost control of the situation and shot dead the occupant of the house. A British soldier had also been killed in the house and it was unclear who was responsible. Quinn was in no doubt that Jacob Candy, the son of one of England's most influential families, wouldn't be charged with anything. The actual details of the incident weren't common knowledge but had been confessed to Quinn by a member of the three man team, who had accompanied the captain into the house.

He just wished he hadn't been told. *Another bloody secret he could do without.*

Life for him had changed so much from when he first set foot in the province. The confident young man so full of good will, who could see clearly what was right and what was wrong and determined to make his mark, was now completely shattered and disillusioned. British informants were on both sides. To Quinn it had become a phoney war with different factions behaving like gangsters, (some were and had become major drug dealers). He was feeling overwhelmed by what he was seeing and hearing. He had started to distrust everyone. He'd been undercover with A14 Field Intelligence Detachment for over ten years, travelling from Sligo, just over the border, to Northern Ireland most weeks, sometimes meeting up with IRA members, in places such as the Bogside, Armagh and Belfast. Even he wouldn't know which of these men were informers. To make matters worse, 14 Field Intelligence were now being accused of collusion with the Protestant paramilitaries. Were the secrets he was passing on ending up in the wrong hands?

To meet his own superiors, different locations, usually in Southern Ireland were chosen. Occasionally he would travel back to the headquarters at RAF Aldergrove. *He knew he'd been in Ireland for far too long.*

Parked nearby, was Quinn's car that was one of the so called "Q" cars. It was a normal looking Ford Sierra, but had hidden

Happy Christmas, 1989

speakers and cameras, with equipment which recorded many of his meetings inside the vehicle. These cars would be fitted with systems to detect any tampering with the electronics, a possible warning that a bomb had been planted in the vehicle. Inside was a hidden Remington rifle 870, so if need be, he could blow the windscreen out, to fire other weapons through it. The vehicle was also armour plated and the icing on the cake was a flashbang dispenser, triggered by a foot switch, where multiple stun grenades fly out in all directions before detonating. This were designed to prevent an ambush. Quinn had fortunately never had to use this option.

His cover identity was John Donnelly, a Dublin born car salesman who the IRA had got to know as a supplier of guns. His breakthrough, when first arriving, had been to meet a Dublin based solicitor called Terry Donaghue, who was in fact a leading light in the Republican movement. It was Donaghue who had introduced him to the IRA hierarchy.

The barman placed the drink in front of him.

"That'll be seventy-five pence."

He lifted the glass to his lips and the coldness of the beer was a relief.

Twenty minutes passed, Quinn checked his watch, it was 6.35pm, his contact was late. Brendan O'Connor was a dairy farmer whose brother had been murdered by the IRA three years earlier and since then, he had kept Quinn informed of many potential terrorist plans and movements. He was worried, for Brendan was a punctual man.

Quinn looked up from the beer he'd be nursing for just over half an hour to kill time. He didn't know it, but another type of killing was about to take place. The pub had started to fill up with drinkers and cigarette smoke. Through the door came young a man, around 25 years of age, ginger hair, freckled pink face, looking very much the archetypical farm boy. He was wearing a heavy woollen green jumper that Quinn could see beneath an open wax coat. *Probably Catholic*, thought Quinn. Farm boy positioned himself at the far end of the bar and ordered a drink. The clock behind the bar showed 6.40pm. Quinn decided he'd give it another five minutes. He looked at farm boy who was looking back into the mirror behind the bar. *Was he looking at Quinn?*

The young stranger started making his way towards the men's toilet situated at the end of the bar just beyond where Quinn was sitting. As he passed, he suddenly drew what Quinn recognised as a Smith and Wesson handgun from his wax coat, and holding it to Quinn's face shouted,

Happy Christmas, 1989

"Happy Christmas, you fockin' Brit bastard."

Quinn leaned back, frozen, he'd been slow to react. Then nothing, the gun had jammed. Quinn had no choice, as the ginger assassin stared looking at the failed weapon and back at Quinn in shocked disbelief, Quinn quickly slid off the stool he'd been sitting on and pulled a Browning revolver from the back of his waist band holster and blew a large hole through the attacker's forehead. Farm boy wobbled a death dance and fell to the floor. The customers in the pub, of all mixed ages, panicked and bundled out through the cage. Quinn followed the exiting crowd and as he came out into the cold night air, he could see outside was a blue Ford Cortina with the engine running, with a driver waiting for farm boy. The car wipers were moving slowly back and forth through heavy snow on the windscreen. The driver stepped out of the car and seeing Quinn alive, reached for his jacket pocket. The drivers' long brown leather coat was covered in an explosion of red as two bullets from Quinn's gun hit him, sending him backwards against the car. He slid down its side onto the snowy white pavement. Quinn walked back inside the pub and waited for the security forces to arrive and just stared at the body of farm boy lying lifeless on the floor. He checked his clothing for ID and it was no surprise to him that he found none.

Quinn knew his time in Northern Ireland was over. His cover had been blown.

Fuck it, he thought.

* These were metal cage structures with a turnstile, to control who came in and out, to prevent groups of gunmen attacking drinkers in a pub or club.

CHAPTER TWO

The Windmills of your Mind, January 1989

Three weeks later in London, Quinn stepped off the train at Baker Street underground station and made his way up Marylebone Road. He passed the statue of Sherlock Holmes and crossed at the lights opposite Madame Tussauds. A few minutes later, he rang the intercom of Mathew Johnson at his rooms in Nottingham Place. (This area is like a small village of private GP's, specialists and psychiatrists. From 6pm, the restaurants, pubs and bars are full of members of this very exclusive club, making referrals for each other. Everyone knows everyone).

"Hello Mathew, it's Michael Quinn," he said leaning into the intercom.

"Ok, I will buzz you in, I'm in the basement," said a rather calming voice.

Quinn went down the stairs and pushed at the white door reading *Mr Mathew Johnson, Psychiatrist.* Johnson was standing inside the doorway. He put his hand out.

"Nice to meet you, Michael."

The basement room was decorated in beige woodchip and sparse, with just two chairs and a small desk in the corner. Quinn surveyed his man. Johnson was around fifty years old with a goatee beard, receding salt and pepper hair, wearing a corduroy suit and unusually shiny brogues, which hinted that he was probably ex-military. He sat down in a large comfortable chair and he beckoned Quinn to sit in a leather recliner positioned opposite him. Quinn sat down, around Six feet away from Johnson who leaned forward and handed Quinn a clip board, on which was a questionnaire with twenty multiple choice questions, ranging from: *do you get heart palpitations* to *do you have suicidal thoughts?*

After filling in the form, Quinn sat in silence as Johnson read his answers.

"Water?"

"Yes, that would be nice."

The Windmills of your Mind, January 1989

Johnson got up from his chair and poured Quinn some water from a glass bottle that was sitting on his desk. Quinn noticed he had a slight limp. *I wonder what the story is with that*, he thought.

He was reading some notes describing Quinn's medical and psychological condition, given by an army psychiatrist and a doctor. PTSD had been diagnosed, a fairly new recognised condition. Quinn filled in the form and waited patiently whilst his new friend read and marked it, almost like it was Quinn's homework handed in to his schoolteacher. Johnsons' expression went from frown to wide eyed surprise as he read Quinn's answers.

Mathew Johnson looked up and gave a faint smile.

"Are you on any sort of medication?"

"No."

He continued to write his notes.

"I understand that just before Christmas you were involved in a serious situation and the army had to get you out of Londonderry.

"I froze and I know, not long ago my reactions would have been quicker. I also would have known my contact being late spelt trouble and I should have been more alert and left. I got lucky."

Johnson looked down at the open file.

"So, what have you been doing the last three weeks, Michael?"

"Just over a week in Belfast at the Palace Barracks, so it wasn't a very happy Christmas, I'm afraid. I was then flown to Norfolt and another two weeks has been spent at Greenwich in army accommodation. and here I am."

"It says here that the night in the pub you were meeting an informer called Brendan O'Connor?"

"Yes, he was a good man. He was found later that night by the roadside, shot through the back of the head and for good measure, he'd been tortured."

"Do you think he gave your identity away?"

"Either that, or it could be the fact that sometimes ex-army come home and join The IRA or UDA and occasionally they cross paths with old colleagues. Surprisingly there's a long tradition of Catholics from Belfast joining the army, from grandfathers to grandsons, right until the troubles. Two weeks before the shooting, I spotted an ex-sergeant in a pub in Belfast, I'd

The Windmills of your Mind, January 1989

known him in Germany, I was sure he hadn't seen me, but maybe he did.

"How do you feel about O'Connor?"

"I feel sad for him and his family. If he did I.D. me, who could blame him?"

Johnson turned back to the front pages of the file.

"You rose quite quickly to the rank of captain. You must have been a good soldier."

"I like to think so."

Johnson read out loud from the file.

"Irish Roman Catholic parents who came here in the fifties. Tell me about your parents Michael"

"Like a lot of young men, my Dad came to England to work at Fords because the eldest in the family would get the farm and the rest were left to struggle. My Dad was the youngest of five. Most men when they came here, would live in digs for a while and then marry a nice Irish girl, they'd either met in Ireland before leaving, or a girl they'd met here at an Irish club. In fact, my parents met on the boat coming over, my Mum came to train as a nurse in Colchester. They married, bought a home in Seven Kings which was to become a strong Irish area and had four boys. Our church, Saint Cedd's was the focal point, along with the Shannon Centre, everybody went there. Church and going to the Shannon were two of the most important activities of the week, apart from Sunday lunch of course! The parish priest was treated with reverence. The women were left to bring the children up and the week culminated with a lot of drinking on Friday and Saturday night. As for my Dad, we never saw much of him, My mum, like a lot of Irish ladies had a strong belief in God and a good education. She made sure we went to a good secondary school, God bless her! My three brothers went to university."

"How did your father take it when you told him you were joining the British Army?"

"He wasn't happy. Like all Irishmen from his generation, they had a dislike of British forces, so the thought of me turning up in uniform, didn't fill him with delight. To be honest, even some of my friends got a bit funny. My closest childhood friend actually threatened me in a pub over a discussion about the IRA. Six years later, he's married and settled with two kids and a cockney accent. I think that's pretty typical. At nineteen you want to take on everyone, at twenty-five, politics is of no interest. You have to remember, the dynamics between the English and the Irish, is a long-complicated love - hate relationship!"

Johnson fiddled with his pen.

"Why did you join the army, Michael?"

After leaving school at eighteen I worked for Lloyds Bank and like a lot of young guys that go into the army, I was bored. But for some it's an escape from unemployment and sometimes a violent broken home. A big part of the army is made up of people that are quite damaged. They train us in war and then throw us into a high-pressure environment to practice crowd control. Do you wonder that things went wrong? I signed up for the Royal Engineers, went to Germany for five years, loved it. It was there I applied to join the Det."

"That's The A14 Field Intelligence Detachment, Northern Ireland, yes?"

"Yes"

"I see out of over nine hundred applicants you were one of sixteen to be accepted into the Detachment in 1979."

"Yes, that's correct."

"Impressive."

"Because of your Irish heritage and Catholicism, were you in conflict about going to Ireland, Michael?"

"No, not at all, otherwise I wouldn't have volunteered. Neither my Mum or Dad were very nationalistic. The nearest my mum came to it was on St Patricks day. At primary school, she'd pin acres of shamrock on us. It was funny looking back, all these little kids covered in shamrock and harps! Don't get me wrong, I'm proud of my Irish roots, but I don't suffer from "plastic paddy syndrome." Anyway, any doubts I might have had as to why we were in Ireland, were soon settled when the IRA started killing suspected informants. I recall one was a mother of ten and when they came for her, the poor bastard thought they were from the Legion of Mary, taking her to safety. She's buried somewhere on a beach. They also liked to torture their victims first, these good Catholic boys and girls.

I have to admit, I thought I'd have maybe three years there and then go onto somewhere in the sunshine. I didn't expect ten years creeping about in the shadows. It wasn't actually seeing the world, was it? But the intel I was getting was so good, it was decided I should stay in there."

"Let me take you back to 1979. What happened when you were first sent to Ireland?"

The Windmills of your Mind, January 1989

"I arrived in Dublin in the July of that year. My cover was to be a car salesman born near the East Wall district, near the docks. I spent three months there learning the streets the pubs, the schools and little things only a local would know. I rode around on a little scooter, getting to know the place. My new identity was John Donnelly. The real one had passed away years ago. My arrival coincided with Thatcher coming to power and was the year Lord Mountbatten was killed by the IRA. On the same day they killed eighteen soldiers at Warren point, so it was quite an introduction.

My first success with the IRA was when I supplied some guns that were supposed to be from the U.S. Over time I got close to them, and I was able to gain information about gun runners, potential targets, IRA members and sympathisers."

"How do you feel about your time in Ireland?"

"I did some good work, operationally."

"Do you think The British Army be in Ireland?"

"I've been asked that several times over the last few years. Everyone thought we'd be in and out quickly, but whether we see ourselves, as peacekeepers or police, we will always be seen by the community as occupiers."

Johnson turned to another page of the report.

"Tell me Michael, I'd like to know if you see paramilitaries as terrorists or soldiers?"

"If the terrorist sees himself as a soldier in a war, all the deaths, including bombs in pubs and shopping centres are collateral damage. You can justify just about anything. Personally, I see them all as terrorists.

One day some years back, I watched an interview on CCTV with a Protestant terrorist who'd just been arrested. He looked like a regular family man, around thirty-five years of age, who candidly confessed that he's just executed a seventeen-year-old lad, simply because he was a Catholic. He showed no remorse, whatsoever. At the same police station, I watched another interview but this time it was with a Catholic who planted a bomb in a pub, calling the innocent victims, casualties of war."

"You don't see it as a war?"

"It can't be, as we are fighting our own subjects, which makes it unique. We are an anti-terror force when it comes to Ireland"

They continued to talk for another half an hour, about his time in Germany and Ireland.

The Windmills of your Mind, January 1989

Finally, Johnson said,

"How would you feel if you were discharged on medical grounds?"

"Disappointed!"

"What would you do?"

"I have no idea; I don't suppose I can put spy on my C.V.!"

"Well Michael our time is up. I will put in writing my findings to the panel, I will be informing them that you are indeed suffering from PTSD and depression, which will require medication. It is for them to decide whether they wish to give you time off or a medical discharge."

"I don't feel depressed, just bloody tired"

"Michael, people don't often realise they are depressed, until they're diagnosed."

A few minutes later Quinn stepped outside. He was in a daze, for it had dawned on him that not only had his time in Northern Ireland come to an end, but so probably had his career.

He flagged down a taxi on The Marylebone Road, that took him to his army accommodation. The cabbie tried conversation, but Quinn was in no mood for small talk.

Later that day, he lay on the single bed in his room that was no bigger than a prison cell. He thought about his life. *What he'd do next, where would he go?* He spent the next two days reading, walking and waiting for a decision on his career.

At 8am three days after his meeting with Johnson, there was a knock on his room door.

"Come in."

The door opened and standing there was a young corporal.

"Captain Quinn, I have two letters for you, sir."

The young man handed him two brown envelopes, saluted and then shut the door behind him. Quinn just stared at them in his hand. He then opened the first letter and read it:

It is with regret we have to inform you that you are to be discharged from your rank as Captain from Her Majesty's armed forces, on medical grounds. Her Majesty's Government would like to thank for your loyal service. British Army HR will advise you of your pension rights.

The Windmills of your Mind, January 1989

The wind was taken out of Quinn. He sat on the edge of the bed, staring at what he'd just read. He read it again and then opened the second letter.

Dear Captain Quinn,

You are requested to attend meeting at 11am on February 10th, at The MOD Building, Room 7 First Floor Horse Guards Avenue , London SW1.

Yours sincerely,

Major John Hadaway.

So that was it then. After fifteen years, I get three lines.

CHAPTER THREE

Queen and Country 1989

A week later, a black cab turned into Parliament Street passing Downing Street, Dover House, The Admiralty and stopped at Horse Guards Parade. Quinn stepped out wearing a light blue suit. For some reason he thought about the day he was promoted to captain. It had been a proud day but being under cover, there was no ceremony, no cheering and when telling his parents of his new rank, on one of his rare visits home, he remembered his Dad saying,

"Oh, very nice. Are you staying for tea?" This was about as enthusiastic as it got!

He stood with the gathered tourists watching the changing of the guard. The winter sunshine flashed against the brass and silver on the horses. The sun accentuated the red tunics worn by the soldiers on horseback. Quinn had forgotten what a colourful ritual this was, he thought for a moment. *If only he'd opted for an easy life like these guards, where their biggest challenge was, which horse to ride, or which girl to take out that evening. How different his life would've been.*

He took a short walk along Whitehall, turning right into Horse Guards Avenue to the Ministry of Defence. He entered the grand hallway of the reception, where there were four women, each with a screen and telephone in front of them. They were all dressed in smart suits. Quinn stood at the reception until one of them came off the phone and looked up. "Can I help you sir?"

"I've come to see Major Hadaway."

"One second, your name sir?"

"Captain Michael Quinn."

The woman picked the phone up and spoke to someone on the other end.

"Room seven, third floor, sir. There's a reception there to report to."

"Thank you."

Quinn walked up a large marble staircase passing bustling men and women, some carrying files, some on large Motorola phones, all seemed to be in a hurry. Some old, some young, some in uniform some not.

As he reached the reception on the third floor, a pretty receptionist said,

"Captain Quinn?"

"Yes, that's me."

"Please take a seat, sir."

He sat on an old green worn chesterfield settee and picked up a copy of The Telegraph. One article caught his eye in particular. It was a story of a Dublin based journalist who had fallen to his death from his apartment window. His name was Patrick Priestly. He remembered the name, as it was the same as one of his cousins, but he also knew the name from a few months back, through one of his informers, that a journalist was doing a piece on the "shoot to kill" policy." Just as Quinn finished reading the article, the receptionist said,

"Captain, they're ready for you now."

He looked up from the paper.

"Please follow me sir," she said with a smile. He followed her and she opened a large oak door.

She walked him through a large bright office roughly the size of a small village hall. It had a high ceiling with two large chandeliers, with a view of the Cenotaph. There was a walk of around sixty feet from the double doors he'd just passed through to a second door which she knocked on.

"Enter," said a rather stern voice.

She stood back and signalled for Quinn to enter. Inside a large interview room, sat three senior army officers, and a clerk to take notes. They sat in line at a polished but weathered wooden table, Quinn didn't recognise any of them. Apart from the young sergeant, they ranged in age from late-forties to mid-fifties. He'd dealt with men like these throughout his career and experience had not left him with a high opinion of such officers.

So, this is it, he thought.

Quinn stood to attention.

The officer sitting in the end of the quorum, didn't look up, removed an unlit pipe he'd been clinching between his teeth and spoke first.

"Do sit down captain."

Quinn sat on a hard upright chair, positioned in front of the four men. It felt like a court setting and he was now at eye level with his inquisitors.

On the table in front of each man was a file which contained both the military and medical records of Captain Michael Joseph Quinn. The second file which they would now refer to, had questions regarding operations in Northern Ireland, past and present.

The clerk looked at Quinn. "Ok if we tape this meeting captain?" It was polite to ask, but Quinn could not really refuse. The machine clicked on,

"This is an interview at 11.10am, February 10th 1990, with Captain Michael Quinn, conducted by Colonel George West, Major Charles Beecham, Major Charles Hadaway and myself, Sergeant Gareth Campbell."

Hadaway looked down at the report in front of him.

"Captain, we asked you here to fill in a few gaps so to speak. Firstly, we would like to ask you about various individuals you may have dealt with in your time in Northern Ireland. Could you tell us your involvement with Sean Kennedy?"

He breathed heavily. In his mind, he could see farm boy falling, that look of shock. He pictured the shooter outside the pub, bloodied and lying in the snow. (Images of past atrocities he'd seen, flashed in front of him). Quinn composed himself as best he could.

"I met Kennedy in 1981. He was a Catholic parish priest at the start of the troubles in 1969. By the time I met him, he'd been highly active for around ten years. Money was coming in from Noraid, but instead of going to the poor it was used to buy arms. He travelled extensively throughout Europe and travelled to Tropoli to meet Ghadafi, who supplied tons of guns and rockets to him. The main weapon of choice was The US Army favourite, the Armalite rifle. He worked with Jimmy Keene, who had been arrested in the 1940's for the murder of a policeman but had been reprieved.

Kennedy would travel to Paris to collect money from the Libyan Embassy and deposit it in a Swiss bank account that the IRA could use, no questions asked. After all, why would you question a priest? Apart from being their money man, Kennedy was good technically. He noticed that a lot of Europeans used a timer called a momo, to be reminded when their carparking ran out. Now several bombers had blown themselves up arming explosives and the use of this simple timer revolutionised their bombing campaign."

"Tell us about your dealings with William Harris?"

"I met Harris in 1983, after a letter of introduction from Kennedy. Harris had emigrated to The U.S. in the 1930's. He was a strange guy, never married, lived with his sister, totally committed to a united Ireland. He would've been, I guess, in his mid-sixties when I met him. Usual thing, more Irish than the Irish. Various high-ranking IRA individuals visited him. He was in constant contact with Kennedy. We set up a sting operation with The FBI to get him for gun running and along with three others, he was acquitted. Although they pleaded guilty, they ran a brilliant PR campaign with the American press portraying them to the public as freedom fighters.

While in the States I met John Mason, an ex-marine who'd set up a gun running network from Boston. He was working with a help of a local gangster called Connor Kavanagh, who already supplied guns to the South Boston Mob, controlled by Jimmy "Butch" Brannigan. These two persuaded local mobsters to "donate." Their biggest shipment in 1984 was seized on arrival in Ireland through information I had gained from Mason. However, I do believe the same source supplied the Semtex for the Brighton bomb two weeks later."

Major Beecham interrupted,

"In 1982 there was The Hyde Park bombing followed in 1984 by the Brighton Bombing. Was there any Intel in advance from your informants?"

"The Hyde Park bombing was carried out by a separate cell, so I had no intel in advance."

As for Brighton, it was again, another small cell, so none of our informers in or out of the IRA got anywhere near knowing what they were planning. Splitting the Brigades up into cells with only the IRA top brass knowing some, but not all of what each cell was doing was clever. Each cell wasn't allowed to share intelligence with each other, so information got tight. At that time our own agent, Steak Knife, was head of IRA intelligence. It was a master stroke, and I have to assume he didn't get wind of what was being planned."

The Major didn't react to Quinn's comment. He turned over another page of the report in front of him.

Quinn could feel the sweat forming around his collar. He loosened his tie and continued.

"Following the Brighton Bomb, the IRA East Tyrone Brigade planned to blow up the police station in Loughall. Four hundred pounds of explosives they carried were from Boston, through Noraid and John Mason. The SAS were waiting for the Brigade, and when the IRA arrived at the police station, the SAS killed nine. You may recall, that was the biggest fatality for the IRA in one day. It was a disaster for them, and they knew internal security had been breached, but thankfully Steak Knife, our agent was put in charge of the IRA investigation. The IRA had gone to all the trouble of creating an internal security unit, splitting different parts of the movement into cells and there was our man, a British agent at the top, even interviewing new recruits."

Again, there was no reaction from the panel.

"I see you were also working with The Force Research Unit?"

"Only in the broadest sense. For agent handling, it really came into its own in Northern Ireland. Within it were members of the army, the Special Branch and MI5. But there was confusion legally as to whether they were fighting crime or at war. That's when the shoot to kill policy blew up in the press and John Stalker investigated and found unarmed men had been shot by the security forces."

"Well, less said the better."

Quinn had heard this phrase, many a time from his superiors.

Colonel West, intervened, "Captain, it says here you had dealings with a loyalist called Derek Campbell."

"Yes, after the launch in November 1986 of The Ulster Resistance campaign, he was entrusted with buying arms. He was tracked to Paris and Geneva where he bought arms to use against the IRA. At the end of 1987, the arms were smuggled into Northern Ireland. The UDA, (Ulster Defence Army), got their share, the UDF, (Ulster Defence Force), lost theirs in a police raid. However, they did get their hands on rocket launchers and grenades. From that point we monitored an upsurge in killings by loyalists."

The Colonel turned another page of the report in front of him.

"And Liam Murphy?"

"One nasty bastard sir. Murphy was in charge of identifying the UDA's targets. He was working for us through the FRU, through their HQ at County Antrim. His job was to pass UDA's secrets on to FRU. He was a former soldier recruited when he was serving time for attacking a blind Catholic man. Within two years he was UDA's head of intelligence. I became suspicious that the army were giving him information to target certain individuals such as suspected IRA members or sympathisers, the opposite of what was supposed to be happening. "

The Colonel didn't respond.

There followed an uncomfortable silence in the room.

"Captain, two men were killed by you in Belfast recently, are you happy you followed the correct rules of engagement?"

"I am sir."

"Any other questions for Captain Quinn?"

There was a quartet of shaking heads.

"Well thank you captain, I'd like to thank you for your service to The British Army, you've been a fine soldier," said Hadaway.

The quartet nodded again in agreement.

A few minutes later, Quinn was standing back outside Horse Guards Parade. A crowd was gathering again to watch the next changing of the guard. In a way it was symbolic. He went to the nearest pub and downed two large scotches and went back to Greenwich to pack.

CHAPTER FOUR

A Quiet Life in the Country March 1999

It was a bright May morning, and like every other morning, Michael Quinn was walking back from the newsagents with the Times newspaper under his arm. He was well known in the village of Applethorpe in Norfolk. With its tannery, antique shops and even a shop that sells outerwear for hunting, it is the type of place Agatha Christie would have felt comfortable setting one of her novels. Very English, gentil, where nothing changes. It even has a 1940's weekend, when they close the roads and everyone dresses in period clothes.

For eight years, Quinn had run Village Vinyl, the record store at the end of the high street. Now 44 years old, he was a bit out of shape. He'd still retained reasonably good looks, not dissimilar to the actor Kenneth Branagh. As for business, it had been slow this year, cd's had been nudging vinyl sales out more and more.

His life was quiet, he drank a little too much, he was still on anti-depressants that got him through the day, but he had finally found some peace in his life. The sleepless nights had gone, along with the PTSD. He'd often think about his days in the army, with incidents playing out in his mind, sometimes in dreams, often at unwanted times. His anxiety episodes came and went. (When they had first started, he genuinely believed he was having a heart attack, it was that debilitating). Despite this, he would describe himself as a fairly happy man, apart from sometimes feeling a little lonely. There had been girlfriends but nothing too serious, but he did like Penny, the new girl from the florist who'd started to call in for a chat and just maybe he'd ask her out. She'd told him she was divorced, and he sensed she'd taken a liking to him. Most mornings he would see her jogging early through the village.

Leaning on the counter of his store, he started reading the paper starting with the back pages with the sports section and then onto the obituaries. That day he was taken aback as the obituary featured an old colleague from his army days. Tom Hammond had been knocked down in London by a hit and run driver, early the previous Sunday morning. Quinn assumed that Hammond had never talked to anyone else about the Londonderry shooting. For it was Hammond that had confessed to him about that terrible night and that he had been the fourth man in the house with Jacob Candy.

A Quiet Life in the Country March 1999

As Quinn looked out through his shop window, he noticed for the third day running, a blue Ford Mondeo parked opposite. Inside he could see two occupants.

What is going on, police maybe, but why?

The shop door opened to the sound of the old-fashioned bell above it.

It was Penny, dressed on a mid-length floral dress, she was a sight for sore eyes.

She smiled and in a cheerful voice and said,

"I hope you don't think me too forward Michael, but the Italian restaurant in the village is launching a new menu tonight and well…, I thought you might like to join me."

Quinn was embarrassed to think she was actually inviting him out on a date. But how could he refuse? He could actually feel himself going red.

"Em.., that would be lovely Penny. I will pick you up at say, seven?

"You know where I live?"

"Yes, Lemon cottage."

"You got it. See you then."

Well, this is a turn up for the books, he smiled.

CHAPTER FIVE

Just a cup of coffee, March 1989

After putting on a suit that hadn't seen the light of day for the best part of five years, under which he wore a white cotton shirt with a tie carefully sculptured into a Windsor knot, which he quickly removed, *too much!* He'd combed his hair back and slipped on his Persol spectacles that he thought, gave him a look of "*rock 'n roller goes dining.* "He dabbed on some Florin aftershave and as he looked in the mirror, he chuckled to himself, *who was he kidding?*

Quinn arrived at Penny's pretty cottage that she was renting, he was five minutes early. As he pulled up in his old car, that he had cleaned especially for the occasion, Penny came out of the cottage without waiting for him to knock.

"Well, I like a man that's punctual," she said.

As she got in the car, slamming the heavy door. He caught a smell of perfume. It had been a long time since he'd been in a car with a date.

Just a cup of coffee, March 1989

She immediately smiled,

"This is like sitting in someone's dining room Michael, what on earth is it?"

"It's a 1969 handmade Bristol 411."

"Well, that means absolutely nothing to me."

"It's got an old-fashioned charm. Always liked them, bought it off a customer who had to give up driving. I hardly use it these days, I wasn't even sure it would start, I should sell it really. "

As they drove back to the village, she kept pressing the various buttons on the dashboard.

Quinn flashed her a glance, "It's like having a little kid in the car!"

They both laughed.

On entering the restaurant, there was a wonderful smell of garlic and the sound of chattering voices. Roberto the owner greeted them with a smile.

"Well, I know who you are, but who's this pretty lady? He took her hand and kissed the back of it. She smiled,

"I'm Penny, Michael's friend."

"May I take your coat?"

She took off her coat and Roberto hung it on a nearby stand. Quinn looked at her standing there in a neat, just above the knee black dress, wearing little makeup or jewellery. She was around 5ft 6", slim with dark features and long black hair. A pretty face, not too thin, quite elegant. The look of an Irish Colleen. Maybe her parentage was Irish?

"You look perfect, said Quinn."

"Well thank you."

"This way," said Roberto.

He led them to a table by the window. Quinn looked around the restaurant. It was almost full, with some couples dressed casually and others looking as if they were going to a dinner and dance. There were not a lot of opportunities to get dressed up in Applethorpe, so some had decided to make the most of "Roberto's Gala Evening."

As Quinn took his seat, Roberto whispered,

"Nice fuckin' suit Michael."

Quinn smiled. As long as he'd known Roberto, almost every other word was "fuckin'."

Just a cup of coffee, March 1989

Most of the diners in the restaurant Quinn knew. Some were his customers, and some were acquaintances. As he caught their eye, most acknowledged him, either with a smile or a slight raised glass, surprised to see him out dining and with a beautiful woman. Antoine from the clothes shop next to the restaurant, waved to Quinn. Antoine had visited Applethorpe twenty years earlier, had fallen in love with the village and stayed. He knew just about every woman in the area, because of his shop selling "couture from Paris." He was feeling a little sheepish as two women in the restaurant were wearing the same "exclusive" dress that they'd bought from him that day.

Penny reached inside her handbag and pulled out a packet of cigarettes. She offered one to Quinn.

"No thanks, gave up a few years ago"

"Wish I could."

She lit a cigarette and waved the smoke away. Quinn pretended he didn't mind her smoking, but he did! Still, he wasn't going to spoil things by lecturing her like all reformed smokers tend to do. Thankfully she didn't light up again during the meal.

A waitress came over with the menu and a specials board. She lit a small red candle in the middle of their table.

"How romantic," said Quinn sarcastically.

Around two hours later, they'd finished their meal, Penny then ordered a dessert, but Quinn decide to order another Peroni. They'd talked nonstop about music, travel, films, but neither had delved too much into each other's past. However, she changed the mood.

"So, Michael, tell me more about your time in the army," she said flicking down on her silver lighter, lighting another cigarette. Quinn had noticed that she had beautiful hands that she used expressively.

Roberto arriving at the table to give Quinn an excuse not to reply.

"Did you enjoy your meal?"

"Superb Roberto," said Quinn."

"It was lovely," said Penny.

"He's an old charmer," laughed Quinn.

"Can we have the bill, once you get over being love struck?"

"Of course."

He went to his little office.

Just a cup of coffee, March 1989

"What about you, what's your background Penny?"

"Brought up in Esher, trained as a teacher, married young. Got divorced, always liked floristry, so here I am! All quite boring really."

"Brief history!"

"Yep, less said the better."

Was she hiding something? Maybe a bad experience?

They continued talking, he was really enjoying her company, she had a lot about her. What he couldn't figure out, was, *what was she really doing in a remote village working in a flower shop in the middle of nowhere?* He hadn't bought her story. It didn't make sense, or was he playing detective a little too much? She was a good listener though. He avoided telling her that his first three years after his discharge had been a long period of recovery, medication and hours of therapy. On top of that, trying to hold down some very menial jobs, wasn't easy. (Like all intelligence who had worked undercover, you leave with no history, apart from the fact that you're ex-army. He'd signed the official secrets act, so he couldn't say what his real role was, even if he wanted to). Still, he had learnt how to flip a burger quite well on a minimum wage!

He talked to her about how he'd always had a keen interest in music, so when the opportunity to take over the shop from the father of an old friend came along, he'd jumped at it. He didn't make much money but with his army pension he got by.

Roberto returned to the table and gave Quinn the bill. Quinn placed the cash with a tip, on a little silver dish and as he picked it up off the table, Quinn said,

"That's fine, thank you."

"Enjoy the rest of your evening." He gave Quinn a mischievous smile.

As they walked to the car, she asked him again,

"Did you say you served in Ireland Michael?"

"No, just Germany and some time in Cyprus."

A few minutes later they arrived outside her cottage. The temperature had dropped considerably. It was going to be a cold night.

"Michael, would you like to come in for a coffee?" She said touching his forearm.

He hesitated; *Does she mean just coffee?*

Just a cup of coffee, March 1989

He smiled,

"Why not?"

Penny opened the front door and they both entered into a small hallway which led to a modern kitchen. The warmth of the cottage was welcome.

"Nice place you have."

"Yes, the owners did it up around six months ago, it was a lucky find."

"Sit yourself down Michael," she said, pointing to a small farmhouse style table.

"Instant coffee, ok?"

"That's fine."

She still had her coat on as she boiled the kettle and filled a mug, adding the coffee and placed the mug and a jug of milk in front of him.

"Sugar?"

"Not for me," he said.

"I will be back in a sec, just got to pop upstairs."

He took a sip of hot coffee. He reached out and added a generous amount of milk.

Quinn glanced around the kitchen. He felt happy and tonight had been the most fun he'd had in a long time. How he so missed fun! *Like being sixteen, things were looking up. Maybe she'd gone upstairs to slip into something more comfortable,* he chuckled to himself.

He continued to sip his coffee, but as he put the mug down a voice behind him said, "Don't focking move, Captain Quinn."

He could feel the cold steel of what he assumed was a gun on the back of his neck. Her well spoken English accent had become a strong Belfast brogue.

"This is for my Daddy and all those you betrayed."

Quinn didn't hesitate, he threw the hot coffee backwards, it exploded onto her face and neck. She grabbed her face screaming. The gun fired as it hit the floor missing Quinn, but shattering the false ceiling, bringing down large shards of Perspex smashing onto the kitchen floor.

She was hysterical, "My face, my face," she screamed.

Quinn shouted, "Where's the shower?"

Just a cup of coffee, March 1989

She carried on screaming. Quinn dragged her up the stairs by her upper arm and found the bathroom which had a power shower in it. He bundled her into it and turned on the cold water. She was screaming uncontrollably. He tore the dress from her. The left side of her face and neck were blistering and he could see that some of the burning coffee had soaked through her clothing reaching the top of her left breast. She stood in the shower her top half naked, turning her face up towards the jets of cold water. He felt bad looking at how she'd been burnt, but he would have felt worse with a hole in the back of his head!

She shouted expletives at him as the cold-water powered onto her. Quinn too was soaked, and despite the abuse, he wrestled with her, pressing a wet towel against her face. After five minutes, she slid to the floor of the shower, pulling her knees beneath her naked scalded breasts, hair bedraggled, just staring defiantly. The elegant woman from the restaurant only an hour before, was almost unrecognisable as the same person.

Quinn threw his sodden jacket into the bath and sat on the edge of it. His shirt and trousers were drenched. He looked down at her, the water still pouring onto her blistered body.

"Look, you are going to need hospital treatment to make sure you don't scar. Alternatively, we can sit here waiting for the intelligence services, who will take hours to get here, which by that time your lovely face might be permanently damaged."

She sat in silence, the water still running onto her.

Quinn dried himself as best he could and spoke.

"You're some fuckin actress, I'll give you that. Who sent you?"

She just glared at him and said nothing. He recognised that look, one he'd seen many a time in Northern Ireland, where the prisoner retreats into themselves. He knew he'd get nowhere questioning her. *She was a pro for sure.*

"I'm guessing, for you to be here alone, this isn't the first time you've planned a killing."

She stared down at the floor, not even acknowledging Quinn's presence.

"Fuck this," said Quinn, out loud.

He went downstairs and dialled for an ambulance on the house phone and while he waited, he picked up the gun that was lying in front of the cooker. It was an AMT semi-automatic, a ladies favourite, for it fits easily into a handbag, yet can do real damage. He knew the gun well, as it was standard

Just a cup of coffee, March 1989

issue for the female operatives in The Det. Her bag was on the work top, which he emptied onto the table. There was a small Nokia 3310 phone, he scrolled through the numbers, but he knew the names would be code names. He checked it for text's, but they'd all been erased. The only other items were a check- in ticket for a morning flight from Stansted to Dublin and a bunch of keys.

As he went back up the stairs, the shower was still running. He pitied her, but this time, she did look up and swore at him,

"You fockin' bastard."

"Yes, you've already told me that."

He sat on the edge of the bath again.

"I now see why you were so interested in my army days. Were you looking for a confession or just planning my last supper? And what's this about your Dad and all those I betrayed?"

Still there was no answer. Quinn spoke.

"You know, I've spent ten years getting away from all the killing and all the hate. What a disappointment you are."

The sound of a siren came through the trees.

She looked up.

"You called an ambulance?"

"Surprised?"

There was no response from her.

The ambulance pulled up outside the cottage, she sat in silence as the sound of the tyres crunching on the stone driveway and the clang of doors opening and a stretcher being retrieved. Quinn let the paramedics in and led them up to the bathroom, explaining that his friend had fallen, spilling hot coffee over herself.

"Lucky you had the presence of mind to get her to the shower mate," said one of the medics.

He examined her face. "What's your name?"

"Helen," she said.

He spoke softly and calmly.

"Well Helen, you've got what I think are second degree burns, but with treatment, you'll be as good as new. Do you think you can walk to the ambulance?"

She nodded, her cold eyes focusing on Quinn, who was now walking back into the bathroom with a dressing gown which he gave to the medic.

Just a cup of coffee, March 1989

"Put this on love," said one of the guys, helping her up out of the shower and covering her half naked body.

He turned to Quinn, "Do you want to come in the ambulance sir?"

"I will follow on thanks."

Quinn walked with them as they helped her into the ambulance.

She didn't look back. Quinn stood in the cold and watched the back lights of the vehicle disappear into the darkness.

Back inside, he picked the keys up off the kitchen table and opened her car up. It was an old Austin Mini, she would no doubt have planned to dump it at the airport. He reached under the seat and he could feel something. It was her passport. He flicked it open and turned on the interior light to read it. Her name was Helen Brady. She was born in Belfast and was thirty-six years old. It had stamps in it from The U.S., South Africa and Dubai.

All the usual suspects, he thought.

He placed the documents back, locked the car and went back inside the house, he searched both floors and found nothing of interest. He left the handbag on the table, with all the contents, returned inside it. He left the gun on the table and then closed the door on the scene of his near execution and left.

He drove back near his home parking his car at the other end of the high street and walked slowly up towards his flat above the record shop. He silently climbed the iron stairs at the back of the shop leading to his front door. In the dark he delicately turned the key and edged the door open. There was no sign of intrusion. He lay awake all night. *Here we go again.*

CHAPTER SIX
The Sound of Music, 1999

The next morning, Quinn walked back from the newsagents in deep thought. Earlier, he'd called the hospital and found out that Helen Brady was recovering well and would be discharged the following day. He was relieved she was ok, despite the fact she had come to kill him, *but why had the IRA come for him, it made no sense?*

He knew the security protocol was that he should have already contacted army intelligence, but he wasn't sure if he could face them, but then again, he was aware he had no choice; he would just have to ring their number. He knew a phone would answer at a desk in Aldershot that would mobilise a chain of events that would lead to the arrest of Helen Brady and lots of questioning.

What caught Quinn's eye as he approached Village Vinyl was the Ford Mondeo parked opposite his shop, yet again. He opened the front door and walked behind the counter and made his way into the back room. He peered through the beaded curtains and studied two men in their thirties as they got out of their car. One reached into the boot and seemed to be looking at something and then put a ruck sack on. They walked towards him; the door clanged as the two men came into the shop. Both were browsing through the film soundtrack section. He had a bad feeling about these two strangers. On the top shelf over the door above Quinn's head, was an old Purdey shot gun that he'd inherited with the shop. He reached up and quietly slid two shells into both barrels and pushing the gun through the curtain.

"Boys, you don't look like fuckin' Julie Andrews fans to me, so I'd like you to keep your hands tightly gripped onto the top of those LP's that you're obviously so fond of."

"We're just browsing mate," said one of the men in a terrible cockney accent, the sort you hear in old black and white British films of the 1950's where they try to sound like Londoners.

Quinn moved within four feet of the men.

"Well Mr Dick fuckin' Van Dyke, who's your mate?"

The other man spoke up.

"Listen, we aren't here to make trouble, we're just looking."

Quinn instantly recognised a Londonderry accent.

The Sound of Music, 1999

"Blimey," said Quinn.

"Two Irish Julie Andrews fans, travelling together through the countryside, how sweet! You wouldn't happen to be looking for Mary Poppins in the form of a lady called Helen Brady, would you?"

Both shook their heads in denial.

"Never heard of her."

Quinn moved even closer to the two men, still pointing the gun at them.

"Well gentlemen may I suggest you leave, right now!"

Both men backed out of the shop and Quinn watched them jog to their car. Suddenly Quinn panicked.

"The fuckin' ruck sack," he shouted to himself.

He ran out through the back of the shop, dumping the Purdey to the floor, and as he reached the back gate of the small rear yard, there was a huge explosion. A rush of air propelled him forward as the blast ripped through the building. Quinn landed on his front surrounded by wood, masonary and fragments of vinyl LP's. The palms on his hands were grazed and bloody as were his knees through torn trousers

As he came to and turned and looked, he was just in time to witness the rest of his shop and flat collapse in on itself. A small fire broke out and black smoke and dust bellowed from the rubble. Water fountained from the mains that had been ruptured. He sat and stared in disbelief and then lay on his back staring at the sky. Everything went silent, the blast had deafened him, then there was a pop in his ears as his hearing returned. Within a few minutes, a crowd had gathered. No one had spotted Quinn, lying at the back of the disappearing building. An ambulance, fire engine and the police all arrived together. The paramedics were the same two men he'd seen the night before and they spotted Quinn. They quickly ran over.

"Not your week, is it?"

They helped Quinn up and he staggered into the back of the ambulance in shock. There was an acrid smell of burnt plastic in the air. The remains of the Sound of Music cover landed in front of him.

Talk about take the piss, he thought.

"How do you feel?" Said one of the medics.

"Fuckin' great" Quinn said sarcastically.

After he'd been checked over, insisting he was *fine*, he was interviewed by the police, who were treating it all as a gas explosion, which was ironic as he didn't have gas to the property. The truth would never come out, British Intelligence would make sure of that. Virtually everyone he knew in the village had come to check on him. Some offered accommodation which he politely refused; Roberto arrived.

"Fuckin' ell Michael, you alright?"

"I've had better days."

"If you need anything Michael, you just say, ok?"

Quinn nodded. Roberto *was a good man.*

After sitting in the back of the ambulance for around an hour, where he made a statement about the two men and the night before with Brady, he stared through the gap of the open back doors. Seven years of work had been wiped out, for what and why the bomb? Why the girl? And why him? In terms of the conflict, he was a nobody. He looked around as the fragments of all his possessions blew about in the wind. He needed help and shelter and there was only one place he wanted to go to.

CHAPTER SEVEN

Home, March 1999

Quinn's parents had moved into a three up two down terraced house in 1953 and forty-six years later, despite most of the community having moved further out into Essex or back to Ireland, they were still there. The influx of Asian families had completely changed the culture of the area. The local shops were now predominantly Asian owned along the high street, selling goods geared up for customers from, India, Pakistan and Bangladesh. The days of the Blarney Stone shop selling all things Irish, had long gone. There was not a soda bread in sight!

Quinn's Mum had often romanticised about moving "back home", but deep down, she knew it was never going to happen. His Dad now seventy-one and retired, was happy enough going for few pints at lunchtime with the few of his old work mates that were left. He'd fell asleep at home until around 6pm, when dinner would be served, usually meat and potatoes in various concoctions. His Mum was an adequate but not good cook. She

Home, March 1999

was no stranger to a Fray Bentos tinned meat pie and Cadburys Smash. She kept herself busy by doing various household chores and would often move the furniture around, which for such a little woman was quite a miracle. Quinn had three brothers and he was the youngest. Two were now living in Sydney Australia, and one Thomas, had recently moved back home after an acrimonious split with his wife.

At exactly 4pm, Quinn pressed the big doorbell he'd first pressed at five years of age. In his hand, he carried an overnight bag with the new clothes he'd just bought. The events that morning had left him with no possessions apart from what he'd been wearing and his mobile phone. Through the frosted glass he could see movement and as his Mum opened the door, she could not hide her delight at seeing her youngest son.

"You're home!" She shouted.

She threw her arms around him which made Quinn feel uncomfortable, for his Mum had never been one bit demonstrative. It also made him feel guilty. Come to think of it, his whole life seemed to be one of feeling guilty about something.

Guilty for not staying closer to his parents, guilty for joining up. Good Catholic guilt, ground in, even maybe born guilty!

"Pat," his mum shouted to her husband, Look who's here!"

His Dad who had been startled out of his afternoon nap, now walked bow legged along the hallway with a smile.

"How are yah son?" He smiled, affectionately patting Quinn's shoulder.

Quinn and his Dad had never been close. There were no memories of football matches he'd played in, with his Dad watching. No holidays to remember, no fatherly advice. As a young child he'd idolised his Dad, pretending he liked the same things. But as Quinn got older, they were quite uneasy in each other's company. *Passing ships*, his mum used to say. Quinn often sensed his Dad felt threatened by his four sons' education. They were all bright boys and maybe he just found the conversation over the dinner table on subjects he knew nothing about, just too intimidating. He was a big simple man, his hair was still jet black, his shoulders hunched from years on the production line. However, Quinn could tell with age his Dad had started to mellow. The three of them sat around an old chipped Formica covered table that had seen many a Christmas and many an argument. Over a two-hour period, Quinn confided his life in the army and what had happened including the previous night's events and the explosion that morning. His parents had

Home, March 1999

been shocked as his secret life was told over countless cups of tea.

Finally, his Dad spoke and put it understatedly. "Well son, it seems you've upset somebody bad enough to want you gone. What are you going to do?"

"Do some digging, to find out what's going on."

His mother looked worried, and she changed the subject in a way that only mothers can.

"Your brother will be home soon, so after dinner, maybe you could go for a drink with him?"

That was always his Mum's magic solution for a problem with one of her sons, would be for one of the others to take him down the pub. There was an irony as she had taken "the pledge" as a child, so alcohol had never passed her lips. Half an hour later Quinn's brother Tom came through the door. On seeing Quinn sitting there he exclaimed,

"Michael, you're back."

"I am indeed," Quinn smiled.

Tom dropped his brief case down on the hall floor and as Quinn went to shake his hand, his brother pulled him into a hug. Tom was a physics teacher, who was now back at home at the age of forty-six, after his wife went off with one of his friends. Six foot tall with a muscular physique and ruddy rugby bashed up features, he had an intimidating presence, but with a real cheeky chappie attitude, and a great sense of humour. Over dinner, Quinn summarised what he'd told his parents to his brother, who asked a lot more questions than they had.

An hour later the two brothers were in The General Havelock pub in Ilford High Street. The pub was big but had seen better days with only four other drinkers in the bar. As an eighteen-year-old, Quinn would be in here with his mates and it would be jostling with drinkers. They'd all meet and then go on to The Room At The Top, Tiffany's or the Birds Nest in Chadwell Heath. Some nights, they'd go to all three.

Tom walked from the bar, and placing two glasses of lager on the table said,

"We're a right couple of saddo's."

"What do you mean?"

"Well, we've got two brothers in Sydney, happy, doing well, kids and all that, and there's you and me. I'm back at home and well, you're a fuckin' mystery to all of us, and just announced you're on some fuckin' hit list."

Home, March 1999

Quinn gave a wry smile, "I see your point."

"Michael, look at this place?"

"What the pub?"

"Well, yeah, but the whole area. Ilford used to be great, it will soon be one massive sad fuckin' pound land. All the nice shops, gone, just more and more chicken and charity shops. I used to come here to buy my stuff from Griffins on the corner and Mr Byrite, it was a treat coming here back in the day."

Tom sat quietly, lost in thought.

Quinn took a sip from his drink, "Changing the subject, what happened between you and Sharon, then? You always seemed the perfect match."

Tom took a big intake of air and sighed.

"As you know, Sharon is a hairdresser, and she comes home one night with the idea of going around people's house's cutting their hair as a bit of extra. So of course, I recommend lots of teachers, including one of my best mates, who's a P.E. teacher. Well, I notice she's going around his house to cut his hair quite frequently, but his fuckin' hair is getting longer and not shorter. Let's face it, you don't have to be Einstein to work out something funny is going on, so I follow her, and of course it's fuckin' Doug, which is his name, that she's getting her bit of extra from, and it wasn't money! So, it's me that ends up at Mum's, and now silly bollocks is in my house, shagging my wife, on my settee, watching my telly and sleeping in my bed."

"Sounds like the three bears!" Quinn said.

"It's not fuckin' funny."

"I'm sorry."

Despite the seriousness of his situation, Tom smiled.

"Like a lot of blokes, I'm out, so we split the house. She got the inside; I got the outside! I walked away with two carrier bags after twelve years together."

Quinn shrugged, "Sorry to hear that, Tom."

"Yeah well, anyway, drink up, I'm depressed enough as it is, it's like a morgue in here, let's get a cab to the Shannon."

Quinn gulped his drink down.

"Blimey, that's a blast from the past."

"Come on, let's get going."

Home, March 1999

They stepped outside and after a couple of minutes, they were walking past the car park opposite the Ilford Palais, (now called Fifth Avenue, previously Tiffany's).

"Ah Michael, the birds I pulled in that place!"

Quinn grinned, "I used to hate that two o'clock in the morning slow last dance. The lights would go up and I'd be standing there with my big red acne face. I bloody hated it. You were always much more successful with girls than me. What I remember about the Palais was the long walk across the dance floor to ask a girl to dance, where the usual response was "fuck off", and then you'd have the walk of shame back with all your mates laughing at you."

"Trouble with you Michael, you were always too shy, too polite and cared just a little too much. Still, they were good days, with many a night spent there and then onto Hungecure after, for a burger or kebab, where most of it would end up on the pavement!"

Tom waved his arm and a taxi pulled up.

"Fuckin hell Michael, look at that," he said looking at the old ABC cinema.

"It only shows Bollywood films these days. I wonder what all the old timers would make of it? Come on, jump in."

THE DERRY SPY

As they rode, Tom leant forward and said,

"Michael, did you keep in touch with your old mate Bob? He was such a great laugh. Never seen a guy who could drink like him."

"Died last year. He went back, home to die at his parent's house."

"What happened?"

"Cirrhosis of the liver. Do you know what? Even after the funeral, the wake at the pub had a "Bobs Bar" and as I walked in, his mum handed me the biggest fuckin' glass of wine I've ever seen. For Bob brought up in a house so full of drink, he had no chance. The eulogy from his brother was lovely though. He said although Bob was the youngest, he was the hub of the family with the biggest heart. Bob had a share in a couple of horses, so would organise race days for all of them and treat everyone. His dad tossed Bob's little lucky mascot onto his coffin at the graveside. I have to admit, it was at that moment I did get a bit choked up. It's funny when he was younger, him and his Dad would hardly talk and yet at his funeral, his Dad looked devastated. We were supposed to have a get together a few Christmas' back and when he didn't return our calls, we thought, fuck him! Turned out, he'd been run over in Wandsworth and was in hospital for seven weeks, typical Bob."

Home, March 1999

Tom smiled, "I remember him at the Lacy Lady when punk night had just started, and the Sun newspaper took pictures of the two of you coming out wearing bin bags. Mum and Dad were mortified, it's a fuckin' McDonalds now."

Quinn smiled and said,

"About five years later, when we'd become New Romantics, I'd arranged to meet Bob in the Coopers Arms, Chadwell Heath, and after about an hour, he turns up, out of breath in full makeup, dressed as a cowboy. He says,

"Sorry I'm late, I've spent the last hour being chased by skinheads around Dagenham!"

Both brothers laughed.

"You know, his party piece would be to dance to "Ain't No Stopping Us Now", by McFadden and Whitehead. Didn't matter, whether you would be in a club, pub or in a shop he'd be doing his little spin, then a shuffle and a clap. Every time I hear that song, I think of him."

The cabby stopped.

"That'll be two quid lads."

The Shannon Centre was formerly a cinema, but with the demise of customers in the 1950's it had become a social club for the growing Irish community. A flight of green sticky carpeted stairs that had seen better days, led to a set of doors at the top, where you would often see someone's bike chained up for safety. On the left was a long bar with a huge selection of spirits. On tap you could get Guinness, Smithwick's, Murphy's Ale and Heineken. There was an assortment of round and long tables with a stage and dancefloor at the far end of the room. By 1999, it was in its last gasp of existence, and its regulars were dwindling by the week.

As Quinn and his brother entered, there was a small group of elderly men all smoking around a round table under a dart board. They all looked up to see the new arrivals. No one acknowledged them.

"I'll get these," said Tom.

Quinn sat down and as he started talking to his brother, behind the bar he saw a familiar face.

"That's our old neighbour Priya Parma. Christ, I haven't seen her in 25 years. I thought she'd moved up north."

"I remember you were mad about her when we were young."

"As kids we used to play together a lot. She grew up and got breasts, all I grew were spots, but she was always nice to

Home, March 1999

me. I used to see her in the clubs and pubs but was always too embarrassed to ask her out. She was the best-looking girl around and all the boys fancied her. Then her folks set her up for an arranged marriage when she was quite young. I remember she went from being around all the time and then she was gone."

"Michael, even if she'd stayed you were never good with girls of any description. I think all boys' secondary schools like ours, made a lot of kids a bit backward with the opposite sex. We used to wonder about you."

"Quinn smiled, "You may have forgotten, but you once asked me at a twenty first birthday party if I was bisexual. I didn't actually know what it meant. That's how innocent I was."

Tom laughed.

Quinn stood up and walked over to the bar where Priya was drying some glasses. She still looked lovely, she was the same age as Quinn, five foot four, long black hair, curvy, but not overweight. She held herself confidently, her generous breasts pushed tightly against a white cotton blouse. Like a lot of Asian women, she looked quite exotic and was still a beauty. Quinn found himself staring at her.

"Well Michael Quinn, what brings you to the bright lights of the Shannon Centre?" She said with the widest of smiles.

"Just back seeing my Mum and Dad and out with our Thomas. It must be what, twenty-five years?"

"Twenty-six actually." Her accent was still London, with a twang of north.

She looked over to where Thomas was sitting, and he raised his glass to acknowledge her.

"I hear Thomas is in my club."

"Which ones that?"

"Oh, you know, the broken marriage, sad story, living back in your old box room club."

"Ah yes, sorry I was a bit slow. What's it like back at home?"

"Well, my Mum and Dad go to bed by 10pm, so when I get in, I have to creep about, so not to wake them up. It's like being a teenager again!"

"How are they?"

"Still in the same house in Ilford since we moved away from next door to you. They are on the lookout for a single, Hindu man, vegetarian, non-drinker, religious and preferably a professional of some sort to marry me off to."

Home, March 1999

"Should be a piece of cake."

"Only if they're about eighty!"

They both laughed.

"Do you know what, I have a confession to make?"

She looked quite serious. "Well go on!"

"I fancied you from the age of about twelve but could never pluck up the courage to ask you out."

She smiled and leant forward "Well I never knew that! "There's still time then." She laughed,

"Michael you're blushing."

"I would fail the non-drinking test straight away! I better get back to Thomas. It's lovely seeing you."

Quinn sat back down at the table with his brother.

"She's still a cracking looking bird Michael. You should ask her out."

"Nah, she's on the lookout for a vegetarian!"

"What!"

"Forget it!"

He chatted to his brother over the next hour, but he found himself glancing over at Priya, more and more. Call it a crush or schoolboy love, but she reminded him of a time long ago before everything seemed to go wrong for both of them.

As the brothers stood up to leave, Priya called over,

"Goodnight lads."

Quinn walked over to the bar and said,

"Could I take your number and perhaps we could have a catch up sometime."

"A catch up? That would be great."

She wrote her number on a small note pad on the bar, tore out the small page and gave it to Quinn.

"Hope to see you soon then," she smiled.

Quinn folded the page and slipped it into his wallet carefully.

The two brothers left and as they turned into their parents road, Tom said,

"Did you know at Fords they used to call Dad the farmer?"

Home, March 1999

"No, why was that?"

"Apparently he used to talk a lot about the farm in Ireland, but I think it was a bit of a piss take, as the farm was a small acreage compared to many of the family farms his mates had come from."

"I never knew that."

"Mind you Michael, Dad had that last laugh. He earnt more money than his mates and older brothers back home, had a great social and working life and was and still is generally pretty happy with his lot."

"I hope so Tom, I really hope so."

That night as he lay in bed, Quinn had to smile to himself. It was he that was in the box room under an old quilt, not his brother. In the distance he listened to the rattle of the night freight trains on the old Southend line, just as he had as a young boy, all those years ago.

CHAPTER EIGHT

Rise and Shine, March 1999

Quinn was lying awake as he heard his mother come into the small bedroom.

She pulled back the Superman curtains that matched his quilt. The bright light hit his eyes.

"Rise and shine Michael, it's a lovely day. I have your favourite ready."

Still blinking, he said,

"What time is it mum?"

"Eight O'clock."

He could smell bacon and eggs, which he could never resist!

Once downstairs, he listened to his Dad slurping tea, reading a copy of The Daily Mirror, without speaking. Quinn ate his breakfast, wearing a pair of his brother's old pyjamas. His mother was ironing with her customary cigarette lodged in the corner of her mouth, pushing her head back squinting as the smoke drifted into her eyes. She'd long mastered the art of smoking and not removing the butt of the cigarette until it was just starting to burn into the filter. Around the house were usually a collection of lipstick covered fag ends sticking out of random ash trays and flowerpots. As always, she was made up, with her dyed black hair neatly tied back. Quinn made small talk with his mother, which included his meeting with Priya. His mother shook her head dramatically,

"Ooh, lovely girl, had a hard time with that man she married. Left her for some young tart, but at least her two boys are grown up now. I still see her mother now and then."

Quinn changed the subject, "Where's Tom?"

He left early and said he hopes to see you later, Michael."

"Not sure what's happening Mum, but if I'm not going to be back tonight, I will call you."

His mother hovered over him with a teapot. She ruffled his hair as she had done when he was little boy.

"Just let us know you're ok, that's all that matters."

After he'd showered and put on new clothes, which consisted of a new pair of jeans, shirt and jumper, he leant on the sink and observed himself in the mirror, he looked tired and felt slightly hung over. He picked up his mobile phone, the front was badly scratched from the explosion the day before. He'd left it on silent and there were eleven missed calls. He listened to the messages, most, were from people he knew, checking he was ok, apart from one from Sergeant David Ross. Ross was a soldier Quinn knew in Northern Ireland who he had contacted on his way to Essex, to see if he could find the whereabouts of Captain Mark Taylor, who with the exception of Candy, was the last man alive from the Londonderry raid. Ross now newly promoted in MI6 was keen to help Quinn, for Quinn had saved his life one night in Belfast, by tipping him off not to go to a planned meeting.

Quinn dialled his number.

A loud voice at the other end of the line said,

"Michael, I've found your man."

"That's great news, what's his number?"

"It's not as simple as that. Captain Mark Taylor tried to hang himself while on leave at his parent's home six years ago. Poor bastard, failed, but was left brain damaged. I don't know how bad he is, but he's in a hospital called Seville's in Surrey. I have the details."

Quinn wrote down the address. Just after he ended the call, the phone rang.

Rise and Shine, March 1999

"Michael Quinn?"

"Speaking."

"It's D.I. John Hunt, Special Branch. Just wanted to keep you up to date. We went to arrest Helen Brady yesterday, but she'd discharged herself before we got to the hospital. There's a warrant out for her arrest."

"Thank you, John, I appreciate you telling me."

Quinn ended the call. *Where had she gone and would their paths cross again?*

Two hours later, his car entered through the large gates of Seville's hospital entrance. A plaque told the world that the building had been opened as The Seville Mental Asylum by his Royal Highness, Edward Vlll in 1936. (He would abdicate only a month later). Nothing had changed much at Seville's in 60 years. Unlike many other of these striking red brick buildings, it had not yet succumbed to closure, and been turned into apartments, but it was probably only a matter of time. Like all these institutions, it was surrounded by large grounds, which was an advantage if a patient got out, because they'd usually get caught long before they reached the perimeter. Quinn accelerated along the gravel driveway that would not have been out of place in front of a grand stately home. He passed a large pond with an ancient fountain, just about managing to spray water. A few patients were working on a section of garden as he pulled up in front of the double doors, over which hung a modern *main entrance* sign, that looked out of place perched on such an ornate building.

"Can I help you?" said a stern looking middle aged woman at the reception, as he walked in.

"Yes, I've come to see Mark Taylor."

She looked down at a list.

"Ah yes, Laburnham ward, second floor. Straight along the corridor, there's a stairs on your left."

Quinn walked along a long corridor that was stark and freezing and looked like it went on forever. The hard tiles under his feet making a loud clipping sound. He climbed an enclosed staircase, and as he reached the second floor, the smell of disinfectant was quite overpowering. A young West Indian nurse stopped him.

"Who are you here to see?"

"Mark Taylor, I'm an old friend."

"Please follow me."

Rise and Shine, March 1999

Quinn was apprehensive as he followed her. She led him into a dark conservatory with large crittal windows. The heavy moss on the glass roof shaded the room from much of the daylight and heavy discoloured lights hung down. Along one side of the room were some soft chairs and in the middle was a mishmash of tables with hard plastic chairs around them. Two white uniformed nurses watched the patients attentively. A large figure in a wheelchair was looking out of the window. His back was to Quinn.

"I have to tell you; Mark suffers from confusion and blurred vision. He finds it hard to concentrate," said the nurse.

She manoeuvred Taylor's wheelchair around, so he now faced Quinn. The figure before him was very different to the handsome officer, fresh out of Cambridge that Quinn had met when he'd first arrived in Germany and had got to know in Ireland. Now around twenty stone in weight, his hair was wispy. He was occasionally making a chewing action on non-existent food; he was a sorry sight. Taylor wore spectacles with one of the lenses covered with a fabric plaster, for he had lost an eye in Northern Ireland, curtesy of a roadside bomb. His head leaned to one side. On his bottom half were pyjamas and slippers, and on his top half he wore an old slightly stained cardigan over a windowpane check shirt that had a frayed collar.

The nurse leant down.

"Mark, an old friend's come to see you."

Taylor lifted his head back and tried to focus.

"Cap…Captain…Q,Quinn?"

"Yes, it's me Mark."

Satisfied that Quinn was a friendly face, the nurse said,

"I will leave you two to chat."

Quinn pulled up a chair and sat in front of Taylor and took out a packet of cigarettes, lit one and offered it to him. Taylor looked over at one of the nurses who was attending a patient who was stroking an imaginary cat.

"They don't really like me smoking, as it's not good for my eye, so they tell me," he said in a whisper.

He slyly took it off Quinn and drew on the cigarette and as he did, he closed his eye and leant his head back. He smiled as he exhaled through his nostrils. The hand holding the cigarette tremored slightly.

Poor bastard, thought Quinn.

"It's been a long time", smiled Taylor, "almost forgotten how lovely a nice ciggy is."

Rise and Shine, March 1999

He spoke with a loud clipped accent, that so many army officers have.

Quinn slipped the rest of the packet into Taylor's cardigan pocket and put his fingers to his lips

"Our little secret," he smiled.

Taylor chuckled, "Well what brings you to my humble abode?"

Quinn was pleased that despite Taylors's disability, he hadn't lost a sense of humour.

"Mark, I've come to see you about the raid you did with Jacob Candy in December 1989 when Davis and the homeowner died. Can you remember anything?"

Taylor rocked back and forth; Quinn could see him thinking.

"Bastards, keep losing my clothes." He laughed.

"Isn't that right nurse?" He shouted across the room. The nurse ignored him.

"Fuckers have got me dressed like fucking Worzel Gummage. What am I a fuckin' scarecrow?"

He coughed and then laughed to himself, holding the cigarette in his mouth and manoeuvred his wheelchair to edge a little closer to Quinn. He was starting to get slightly manic.

"Mark, we were talking about that night in Londonderry, the raid."

"We should have told, Candy panicked, shot Davis and the Irishman. The bastard warned us, if he went down, we'd go with him. We were scared and the longer we kept quiet, the worse it got."

Quinn leant forward in his chair.

"Mark, are you saying Jacob Candy shot both Davis and the owner of the house?"

Taylor was trying to focus. It was if the air had been let out of him. Suddenly he was hunched, leaning forward, twitching.

"Who did you say you were?" Said Taylor.

Quinn moved his face closer to Taylors'.

"I told you Mark, it's Quinn, remember, we met in Germany and then Ireland?"

Taylor was looking more confused. His right foot was nervously tapping up and down on the footplate of the wheelchair.

Rise and Shine, March 1999

"Headaches. I..I g.. get terrible headaches."

"Mark, please focus. Are you telling me, that night Jacob Candy killed both men?"

"Murder. It was murder"

Taylor said it loud and clear. He suddenly smiled with a look of triumph. As if somehow, through that jumbled mind, he'd managed to push out a naughty childish secret.

His shouting alerted one of the nurses and she came over.

"I think Mark needs a rest," she said protectively.

"Of course."

She took the cigarette from Taylor's fingers. You know smoking's not good for you Mark."

Taylor looked down at the floor as if he was a scolded schoolboy.

She looked disapprovingly at Quinn, who clasped Taylor's hand.

"Mark, it was good seeing you."

Taylor had slumped his head forward onto his chest, he had fallen silent. His eye was closed. He looked lost in his own world that he had retreated into. As Quinn stood up, Taylor lifted his head.

"He was here you know."

"Who?"

"Candy."

"When?"

"Two, maybe three weeks ago."

"What did he want?"

Taylor manically scratched his head.

"I don't remember, I wasn't in the mood, don't like him anyway," he said coyly.

What was Candy up to? Was he here to assure himself of Taylor's state of mind? Thought Quinn.

He put his hand on Taylor's shoulder,

"It's been good to see you, Mark. I will come and see you again."

"Sure, you will," he said disbelieving and smiled a wide smile.

Quinn felt sad for Taylor as he walked back along the corridor.

Rise and Shine, March 1999

As he reached his car, he crouched for a moment. From the pit of his stomach, up through his lungs, that godawful feeling grabbed him. Suddenly the pressure was building up inside him. Was it what he had seen or heard, or was it that just about everything was overwhelming him?

"You alright sir?" said a voice behind him.

He turned and saw a young nurse who'd just arrived for a shift looking concerned.

"Oh yes fine. Just had, you know, a bit of a shock."

She nodded and smiled, acknowledging his explanation and carried on walking.

What should he do now? The information he had about Jacob Candy was explosive. Why had he killed Davis? At the same time, officers involved were being targeted by what seemed to be an IRA hit squad. He didn't particularly care if they got to Candy, he deserved it, but he wasn't going to sit around waiting for another visit from them. He took out his phone and scrolled down to one of the few numbers he'd kept from his days in Ireland.

"Seamus, it's Michael Quinn, I need a favour…"

CHAPTER NINE

Sister Mary Comes to Me, March 1999

Quinn looked down as the plane flew over Irelands Eye, a familiar island landmark just off the east coast of Ireland. The lights on the buildings were just coming on as night descended. The wheels hitting the tarmac made the plane shudder and the recorded message announcing that another Ryanair flight was ahead of schedule sounded over the intercom. As Quinn walked down the plane steps, the wind caught and flapped his open coat. It was a relief to make the shelter of the terminal and it also felt good to be back after all these years. As Quinn approached passport control a border guard smiled and said, "Welcome home."

He smiled to himself, *Jesus, do I look that Irish?*

Exiting through the sliding arrival doors, his old contact from the Irish police, Seamus Kelly was waiting, leaning over the barrier for a warm grip of a handshake.

Sister Mary Comes to Me, March 1999

"Thanks for coming out to meet me this late Seamus."

"Think nothing of it. I get calls from ex-British Army captains all the time, asking me to urgently meet them. Have to admit, I'm intrigued."

Seamus Kelly was sixty years of age, tall with an impressive beer belly that pushed against straining shirt buttons. He had a mass of greying windswept hair on top of a big red face, that made him look like he belonged on a fishing boat rather than in a police car.

The two men walked to Seamus' old Ford Focus in the multi storey car park.

"Blimey Seamus, you been banger racing"

"Listen, you can walk if you like."

"No, it's just I've never seen a car with that many dents since I was a kid!"

"Where we off to then?"

"I've booked The Shelborne."

"Very posh."

They headed along the N7 towards Dublin city. It was nearly midnight.

THE DERRY SPY

"What's going on then, Michael?"

"Seamus, I believe there's some sort of republican hit squad targeting me and officers that were involved in a raid that went wrong in eighty-nine. Two are dead, one's in a mental home and the other is now an MP with political ambitions and still alive as far as I know."

"Well, I found the information on your lady you asked about. She lives here, in the city. No criminal record, she works in a travel agent's in Dublin. But this is the best bit, and you're gonna love this. She's an ex nun."

"You're fuckin' kidding me!"

"Nope. From the age of eighteen until twenty-six, she was none other than Sister Mary, teaching in a Catholic primary school in Donegal. The shooting of her father, Derek Brady by a British soldier, caused a drastic career move on her part. She's a dangerous lady Michael, but neither us or the RUC have ever been able to pin anything on her. We think she got to one of her victims by dressing up in her old nun's outfit. Who wouldn't let a poor nun into their house?"

Quinn thought for a moment. "Fuckin'hell Seamus, she's Derek Brady's daughter! The British soldier that killed her father was Jacob Candy!"

Sister Mary Comes to Me, March 1999

"But why target you, an A14 officer who wouldn't be on a raid."

"That's what I don't understand."

Quinn noticed Seamus constantly looking in the rear-view mirror.

"Two little fuckers on a motorbike. They've been behind us since we left the airport," said the big man.

Quinn looked over his shoulder, the bright head light of a Goldwing motorbike shone at them.

Seamus pulled the old Ford sharply into a country lane, the tyres squealed, but the Goldwing followed them He could see the bike closing in and then moving alongside, with two passengers both in black leather jackets and salopettes. As the light reflected off the car, Quinn could see the stock of a machine gun being retrieved from one of the bikes panniers.

"Look out Seamus!"

There was an explosion of glass as gun bullets hit the old Ford. Seamus' head slumped forward ramming against the centre of the steering wheel. The horn sounded continuously under the pressure of his face. The rush of air blew through the cars shattered windows. Quinn frantically grabbed at the steering wheel. The back off- side tyre blew out and the car careered off the road and up a grassed embankment, slamming against a large oak tree. On impact, Seamus' lifeless body rocked forward and then back and was now wedged with his head resting between the two front seats. His mouth was open, his face contorted, blood was running from two holes, one in his right temple and one in his cheek. Somehow Quinn had missed being hit.

Steam hissed out of the smashed front end of the car. Apart from Quinn, a lone streetlight was the only witness to the Goldwing turning round and then stopping, with one of the riders getting off, no doubt back to finish the job. Quinn hurriedly opened up the glove box. He found what he was hoping for.. *Thank God.*

Seamus was Garda old school. *"Always keep a backup in the car, wherever you are going, in case of attack."*

Quinn pulled out an old Webley revolver that Seamus had rammed into the glove box. As the passenger from the bike walked up the embankment in the dark, Quinn could see the outline of a small automatic machine gun in his hand, pointing at the ground. The rider had assumed Quinn would be either dead or unconscious and climbed the embankment towards the car. Quinn rolled out through the passenger door and with one shot, the man's white helmet

Sister Mary Comes to Me, March 1999

punctured. The assassin's feet lifted off the floor and he lay lifeless on the muddy bank. Quinn got up and ran towards the driver of the Goldwing, still sitting on the bike. Quinn fired twice, the black figure swayed and toppled and as he fell, the bike keeled over on top of him. Quinn walked over to the lifeless body and pulled the riders helmet off, revealing a male of around 40 years of age, black short hair, hard features. It was one of the bombers from the day before. He searched his body for ID but there was nothing. He walked up to the passenger lying on the embankment and rolled him over. This was a male of around 35, shaven head, broken nose. It was "Mr Dick Fuckin'Van Dyke", as Quinn had called him.

What was going on? He hadn't been in Ireland more than an hour and someone was already on to him, and a good friend was dead. Quinn pulled out his mobile phone and called The Garda.

After two days in custody, Quinn was released with no charges. The police had done their various checks and had no reason to detain or deport. The questioning from The Garda had been extensive and it was only when they were satisfied that he was the victim and not the instigator of the attack, that they were willing to set him free. They had after all lost one of their longest serving officers, so Quinn understood their ire.

A police car dropped him off at The Shelborne, Dublin's most famous hotel. It's a large Victorian building, opposite St Stephens Green. As he entered the front revolving oak doors, the receptionist stared at what she regarded as a scruffy intruder. She glanced back at her manager, who on seeing Quinn, thought it best to take control of the situation.

"Can I help you?" he said, sniffily looking at Quinn, standing there, in the grand marble reception, looking like he should be collecting for the homeless.

"I have a room booked in the name of Michael Quinn."

The manager looked at his screen disbelieving. He pursed his lips and with a look of surprise said,

"Ah yes, I see you rebooked this morning."

"Forgive my appearance, there was an accident on my arrival, which is why I'm two days late."

Satisfied with Quinn's explanation but still suspicious, the manager said with a patronising tone,

"Would sir like his bag taken up?"

"No, I'm fine, just got the one holdall," he said, holding it up.

He took his key and made his way up to his room and stood just inside the doorway throwing his bag onto the

Sister Mary Comes to Me, March 1999

bed. He ran the bath and after walking out of his muddy stained clothes, he lay in the bath drinking a large scotch he'd taken from the mini bar. His legs and upper body were bruised from the impact of the crash. He thought about poor old Shamus. He'd only come to do Quinn a favour and now he was dead.

After drinking a second scotch, he dozed off and abruptly awoke two hours later by the coldness of the water. After getting dressed, he went down to the reception, taking a free map off the desk, he sat with another drink in the Horseshoe Bar. Apart from the barman, he was alone. It was just after 2pm. The barman noticed him looking at the map.

"Do you wish me to mark some of the sights for you sir?"

"No, it's ok, I know the city quite well."

Quinn turned left out of the hotel and made his way up Merrion Street. The day was bright, he passed the science gallery and then walked over O'Connell Bridge. Dublin had changed a lot since his days of driving around the city memorising streets on a moped. To him, it was as if the Irishness of the place was being replaced by a generic European look. He dropped some coins into a busker's cap and passed under Clerys clock where just about every courting couple in Dublin, have all met at one time. He caught the lift up to the café on the top floor and ordered tea. When he'd first arrived in Dublin all those years ago, he'd spent hours studying maps at the very same table he was now sitting at. He looked up and smiled watching an old guy in a trilby smoking a cigar directly under a *No Smoking* sign.

Quinn laid out the map on the table. He wanted to refresh himself as to the bus routes.

"It's John, isn't it?"

He turned, to see an elderly lady with blue rinse hair, he vaguely recognised. It had been a long time since anyone had called him by his pseudonym, John.

"I see you're still pouring over those maps."

He smiled at the old lady, and she continued,

"Forty years I worked here, retired last year, still miss it. That's why I come in once a week."

"Well, it's lovely to see you," said Quinn.

He watched her make her way to the lift. She turned and waved, and he waved back with a smile.

Sister Mary Comes to Me, March 1999

The walk from Clerys to Brady's office in Parnell Street, is around five minutes. He sat in The Rotunda café in the park opposite.

Quinn checked the time it was 4.30pm. Just after 5pm he spotted Brady. She had obviously recovered from her burns. She looked like she was in a hurry. He followed her as she walked along O'Connell Street and waited at bus stop. Quinn kept his distance and waited for her to get on and he followed. The bus was busy, so he hung back towards the rear of the vehicle.

The bus wound its way through Dublin and at a stop in West Road, she got off.

Light rain had started to fall and it was now twilight. Quinn turned up the collar of his coat, following at a distance.

The East Wall district of Dublin was once a Protestant middle-class district, but now it was a grey run-down area of private landlords renting to mainly eastern Europeans who work in construction and the care sector. Helen Brady turned into a small cul de sac and reached into her handbag for her house key. Quinn waited on the entrance to her road and waited for her to enter a small grey pebble dashed house with green iron railings to the front of the property. On the driveway was a blue Fiat Strada.

Time to confront her, he thought. He quickly crossed the road and walked up to her front door and rang the doorbell.

She opened the door and with no look of surprise, and as if meeting an old friend, said,

"Do come in Captain Quinn."

As he stepped through the door, something sharp pressed into his neck and darkness came over him.

CHAPTER TEN

Welcome to Dublin, March 1999

When Quinn awoke, he felt a soreness where a needle had entered. For a moment he thought he must be in hospital but as he came round, he realised he was in a very old bedroom. He focussed on the wallpaper that depicted little Chinese figures in a field. It was dream-like as it reminded him of his grand-parent's wallpaper in their house in Cork. Every summer his parents would take him there to stay. He'd sit there, seen but not heard, staring bored out of his wits, at that bloody wall.

He was freezing and naked, with his hands and feet cabled tied, sitting on a wooden chair. The floor rustled, he looked down and could see it was covered in polythene. He often thought it may end like this, but that was when he was younger, in the past, but not now.

He heard a voice behind him. "Ah, you're awake, English. Welcome to Dublin, the sedative we gave you was a bit stronger than we tort."

It was a deep nasal Dublin accent. A tall male around fifty years of age, receding black hair with a pock marked sweaty face, slammed a chair in front of Quinn. The back of the man's chair was facing Quinn and he sat on it astride.

"Welcome to Dublin, Captain Quinn of the fockin' Brit Army."

"And your name?" Said Quinn, as he shivered from the cold in the room.

"Don't think you need to know!"

The big man theatrically pushed his sleeves up, as if getting ready for a fight.

"I feel I recognise you from somewhere. You ever been up in the North?"

"Many a time English, but I'm sure I'd remember a bastard like you. I assume you know what comes next?"

"You promise me that if I tell you my secrets, I get to go home, but we both know that doesn't happen."

The interrogator moved his face close to Quinn. Quinn could smell he'd been drinking. *A bit of Dutch courage to get the party started, maybe?*

"I do love a clever Brit bastard."

Welcome to Dublin, March 1999

He stood up and suddenly swung at Quinn, putting his full weight behind the blow which hit Quinn square on the mouth. His head rocked back; he could taste blood on his tongue.

"I've interrogated men a lot harder than you, Captain Quinn, and by the time I'd finished with them, they're crying for their mammy."

The door opened and Helen Brady entered and placed a chair next to the big man's and sat down crossing her legs to calmly watch the proceedings.

"I see you've started already Bryan!"

It confirmed to Quinn, that if she's happy to use the big man's name, it definitely means that they're not expecting him to leave alive.

He could see laid out on a little table behind them, various tools including plyers, cutters, a hammer and other basic interrogation aids. On the right of the tools was a handgun. Next to the gun was Quinn's Rolex Thunderbird, a watch the army had supplied to compliment the illusion of the affluent gun dealer. It was the one thing he'd kept from his time in Ireland.

Brady crouched down and put her face close to his.

"I bet you hoped we might get naked that night at my place, eh Michael."

She placed her fingertips under his chin and lifted his head slightly.

"Naked, but not tied to a fockin'chair eh?" She laughed, and nodded to the big man, who then hit him with another punch across the left side of his face. Quinn spat some blood out from his mouth. He looked at Brady.

"I take it you have friends in the Garda that told you I'd arrived in Dublin?" He lisped through swelling lips.

"We heard you were coming and assumed you'd come looking for me, so we simply had you followed. Pretty dumb on your part, coming here, you made it almost too easy for us."

"The man you killed, was a good friend of mine."

"We didn't mean for one of the Garda to get killed, however, let me tell you about killing Captain Quinn.

"You and three other British soldiers, come into our home and shot my Daddy. So, I know all about killing."

He slowly raised his head and stared at her, breathing heavily. *How was he ever going to get out alive?*

Welcome to Dublin, March 1999

"I was never in your house," he gasped.

"I was A14, so there's no way I'd be on a raid."

The big man came forward almost running as if bowling a ball, hitting Quinn with another heavy blow.

Quinn rocked back and forth. The cable ties were cutting into his wrists. *So, was this how it was going to the end? Slumped in a chair, head on his chest with blood running from his mouth dripping onto his naked body*. Brady sat in silence for a few moments. Quinn stared at the big man.

I know him but where from? He thought.

Brady got up and paced up and down.

"I don't intend to make this last for long. We are after the names of informers that worked with you and it will be over, either painfully or without pain."

"If you want me to name informers, we'll be here all night, cos it's probably about half the IRA membership!".

The big man clenched his teeth and fists ready to attack again,

"Funny focker, aren'tcha?"

Brady held her hand up and said,

"Stop!"

"He's no good to us if he can't talk."

Quinn looked up. "What I will tell you, is that the men that night in your house, were Captain Hammond, dead, Captain Taylor, in a mental home, and Sergeant Davis, dead. The raid was led by an officer called Jacob Candy. Candy shot Davis and your father and it was covered up." (The only name he'd given away who'd be vulnerable was Candy).

Brady walked over to him, leant down on his shoulders, her face close to his.

"Who the fock is Jason Candy?"

He looked at her expression. *She really didn't know who he was?* There would only be one reason that Candy wasn't on the list, he must be creator of it.

"I think your people have been set up to kill British personnel to protect Jacob Candy, ex-Army captain, MP and your father's killer.

She looked agitated, "No way, no fockin' way." She shook her head.

Quinn could see, she wasn't totally disbelieving him. She felt confused as to what Quinn was saying as it had a ring of truth.

Welcome to Dublin, March 1999

He'd cast doubt in her mind. The big man was standing with his back to the curtained window with his arms folded not saying anything, ready to attack, just listening, watching and sweating.

Quinn continued, "Can't you see the irony? The IRA assassinating people on behalf of the British Government."

Without warning, the big guy moved and swung a blow catching Quinn's right eye, knocking him and his chair backwards onto the floor.

The interrogator leaned over him, fists clenched, face, red with rage

"Fockin' liar! You think we're fockin' stupid English?"

Brady shouted,

"Wait."

"Pick him up."

He pulled Quinn up off the floor, still attached to the chair by cable ties. Quinn could smell the big man's body odour.

Quinn's eye socket blew up with the swelling. Blood oozed over his bottom lip onto his chin.

She turned to the big guy.

"Stay with him, and don't hit him anymore. I've a contact I can call."

The two men looked at each other.

Suddenly Quinn realised who he was. After a few minutes Brady returned.

"The big man turned to her,

"Well?"

"We need time to speak to the leadership to decide what to do with him. We need him alive."

The big man was agitated. "No, this Brit bastard dies here."

Quinn looked at him.

"I know you. You're Bryan O'Connell, Michael Adams' lieutenant in Ulster for years. You had his ear but unfortunately for him, British Intelligence had yours."

"Brady looked at the big man. Is this true? Murphy was shot by the Para's in an ambush. Was that you're doing?"

"Now listen Helen, and as he stepped forward, she grabbed the revolver off the table and pointed at him.

"How would he know you worked for Adams if it isn't true?"

"He's probably seen my file somewhere."

"You seem too keen to finish him off."

"You don't understand Helen."

He grabbed her arm, but as she tried to struggle free, the gun went off, a spray of blood flew up onto the magnolia wall and he fell towards her like a manikin cut from its strings, floppily hitting the floor face down with a sickening thud. She dropped her arm holding the gun to her side. Her other hand, she held over her mouth in shock. Blood pumped over the polythene and reached Quinn, warming his bare feet.

She stayed calm despite of what had just happened.

She turned to Quinn and raged at him.

"You better not be lying. I've been fighting you fockers for years and just when I think we are getting justice, now this, killing for the fockin' Brits. She slumped down, with her back against the wall. She didn't cry, she was just completely still and silent.

"We were informed about you by a contact we have in London. All I know is he supplied the leadership with the names of ex-military to hit. We only knew him by a code name, "Danny Boy," do you know him?"

Quinn was in pain, the sort of pain where your body feels empty and literally every part of your being hurts. he looked at her.

"I don't, he gasped," but I can find out if I can get back to London."

She pulled herself up, using the edge of the table and picked up a Stanley knife.

Quinn bridled in the chair.

"Don't worry, I'm not going to cut your balls off, just the cable ties."

She stepped over O'Connell's body and walked across the blood pool that was now covering most of the polythene. She stared at the body on the floor and matter-of-factly said,

"It's amazing how much blood comes out of the human body, don'tcha think."

"Must admit, I've never really thought about it."

Welcome to Dublin, March 1999

Quinn rubbed his wrists as the cable ties were cut off.

She stood back and threw the knife onto the table.

"Your clothes are in a bin bag in the bedroom next door. She raised her eyebrows as Quinn shuffled passed her, naked and trying to keep his balance.

"We assumed you wouldn't need your clothes by the time O'Connell finished with you."

Red footprints followed him into the bedroom. He was in agony as he wiped the base of his feet on an old candlewick bedspread and slowly got dressed. It still amazed Quinn, the pain some humans are willing to inflict on others in the name of religion or whatever the reason.

He stood at the top of the stairs; Brady looked at him.

"Can you get the keys to the car out of his pocket? I don't want to walk across the floor again."

Quinn stood over O'Connell's body and reached into his trouser pocket and took out the keys to the Fiat. From off the table, he retrieved his watch and slipped it over his cut wrist.

"We need to get going. We've maybe got a couple of hours until he's discovered," said Brady.

She steadied Quinn down the stairs.

An hour later, they parked up behind The Shelborne.

The same receptionist from that morning, looked at them with shock.

"He got hit by a car, but he'll be ok," said Brady.

"Do you have a first aid box?"

She went into a back office and handed a red canvas bag with a cross on it, to Brady.

The receptionist gave the key over, staring a Quinn's battered face. It occurred to him that she was probably wondering how this guest was so fucking accident-prone! They caught the lift and in Quinn's room, Brady helped patch him up as much as possible.

He sat on the edge of the bed sighed, exhausted. He noticed how cold and in control she seemed.

"Listen Quinn, you need to get out of Ireland tonight. If you don't, you won't get out alive. Once our boys find O'Connell back at the house, they'll assume it was you that killed him. I'll tell them you dragged me with you and I escaped as we got into the city."

"Will they believe you?"

Welcome to Dublin, March 1999

"Of course."

She put her coat on and said,

"I'll catch up with you in England. If Candy is responsible for my Dah's death, he will pay. If you've lied to me, well…."

She didn't have to finish the sentence for Quinn to understand what she had in mind for him.

He booked the last flight out to Stansted and packed his few belongings. A cab picked him up outside the hotel.

The cabby looked at him.

"What the fock happened to you?"

Car accident mate, said Quinn.

The flight was the usual assortment of mainly business travellers who'd been in Ireland for the day.

At passport control, the staff looked at him closely, but no one stopped him. Despite the dark glasses he'd bought from duty free, his swollen face and lips attracted too many glances for his liking. A small child had stood on her seat staring at him.

Around 1am, he arrived at his parents' home, they were in bed. He sat at the kitchen table, trying to drink a beer with difficulty. His brother Thomas came down from upstairs.

"What the fuck!" He exclaimed.

Quinn went through what had happened since his arrival in Dublin.

"Michael, what have you got yourself into?"

"I've got to see it through Thomas."

The next morning the familiar swish of the curtains sounded and his mum saying,

"Good morning, Michael" She went to wake him and saw the state of his face.

"Bee Jesus what's happened?"

Quinn was still fully dressed under the covers.

"It's a long story Mum, he mumbled. I just need to rest for a bit, and I'll be fine, don't worry."

"At that moment, he started to weep uncontrollably. His mother leant over the bed and embraced him.

"My poor boy, what have they done to you?"

Welcome to Dublin, March 1999

She brought him up a tea but the damage to his mouth made it impossible to drink. His whole body ached. His face and lips were sore and one of his eyes was badly blood shot.

"Now you stay here as long as you like," said his mother.

After taking some pain killers and his usual medication, he went back to sleep. Over the next few days, his dad would come and sit on the end of the bed, just sitting there in silence. There was then a pattern of sleep and watching TV of an evening with his parents.

"Just like the old days," his Mum would say every night as she loaded him up with even more scones and bad T.V.

After 12 days, his face had healed but he was still feeling fragile and with his mother's fussing, felt about five years old.

It was a Sunday morning and Quinn decided he'd go for a walk. After an hour he arrived at St Chad's park an old haunt of his as a kid. (Ironically a British soldier on leave, had been killed in this park a few years before).

He passed the once pretty flower beds that were now muddy and empty, and he sat at the derelict club house by the tennis courts with rusting chain link fences, where he'd played almost every Saturday with his mates. As he walked towards the far end of the park, he noticed the once loved back gardens were now just storage areas for people's old mattresses and abandoned car and bike parts. Gone was the pitch and putt course and the famous paddling pool was now dry and cracked? *So, this was what progress looks like.*

He remembered how the old ladies in the high street cottages used to stand in their tiny front gardens talking over the fence and people watching. All were swept away for the development of a supermarket. *Was it just him, or did things seem better as all those years ago?*

Later when he arrived back at his parent's home, his mother called out to Quinn,

"Michael, there's a friend of yours here."

As Quinn went to the kitchen, sitting there, eating a large breakfast, he probably didn't want was Sergeant Ross. His mother smiled,

"I'll leave you boys to chat."

Ross put his cup down.

"I got your message you were here. Look Quinn, I think the MI6 are on to you. I got asked yesterday by my

Welcome to Dublin, March 1999

commanding officer, if I'd heard from you recently. I said you'd phoned, and I'd called you back as you were asking about funeral arrangements for Captain Hammond. It could be, that they found out you visited Taylor in hospital, and they will know by now about what happened in Ireland. I owe you my life, but If I do anymore, it could end my career."

"Don't worry Ross, it was good of you to come here."

"Well, I dare not speak over the phone, as I'm sure they will now be listening to my calls by now.

Ross took out a file from the sports bag he was carrying.

"I do have a parting gift for you though."

He handed over the file to Quinn.

"Do you remember Frank Bufee sir?"

"Of course. French Dad, Irish Mum, arms buyer for the UDF. He knew me as John Donnelly."

"Not long after you left Ireland, he disappeared, and everybody assumed he was dead. In that file, you will see that he was working with Candy who got him a new identity through MI6. I've managed to get his relocation address in France, It's in there. You might be able to get some information out of him, as by reading that file, it's obvious that Bufee and Candy worked closely at one time. By the way, he now calls himself Francois."

"Very French. David I do appreciate the risk you've taken."

Ross stood up,

"Text me if you're in trouble. One other thing, you asked what Jacob Candy's codename was . It was changed after you left Londonderry. It was Danny Boy."

Quinn leaned back into his chair in thought.

"Well, well."

"Does it help?"

"Just confirms something I already thought I knew. By the way, when is Hammond's funeral?

"It was yesterday."

"Oh, I'm sorry to have missed it."

"One other thing Quinn, try to use cash as much as possible. Every time you use your bank card, your movements are traceable."

"Thanks David, as you know I'm a little rusty, so I appreciate the tip."

Quinn's mother came into the kitchen.

"Now how about a nice cup of tea and a scone for you two, they've just come out of the oven."

Ross smiled and sat down again and said,

"Go on then, it would be rude not to!"

CHAPTER ELEVEN

Lost in France April 1999

The following morning, after a long bureaucratic ritual, Quinn managed to draw £2000 from Barclays Bank.

The next day he flew out from Gatwick, and on arrival, picked up a car from the rental office at Toulouse airport. As he walked to the car park, the intense heat so early in the season, took him by surprise. He'd taken the 7am flight and it was now 11am as he pulled the car out onto the motorway. Toulouse is a difficult city to get out of, with its multiple roundabouts and intersections. Quinn followed the map as best he could but found himself going around two roundabouts twice. At Cahors he pulled over for a coffee and took his jacket off. (Before all the motorways were built, the town was a major stopping off point for Brits on their way to the South of France. (An old chain-smoking acquaintance of Quinn's, had worked as a mechanic there in the sixties and had told him stories of British tourists delighted to find an Englishman to repair their car).

Lost in France April 1999

From Cahors he then took the road to Vers and then through the villages, Bouzies, Tour-de-Faure, Larnagol, and finally Calvignac. The village is nestled on a hillside, overlooking the River Lot. Quinn found Frank Bufee's house on the road leading to a cemetery, which was on a small hill, surrounded by a stone wall. Quinn pulled in slowly onto the gravel drive, which wrapped around the rear of the house. There was a large swimming pool, that had an assortment of parasols and sun loungers around it. The house itself would have been originally a single floor property with a basement, but Bufee had dug it out to create two floors. Next to the house was an old barn used to keep their vehicles out of the hot sun.

Quinn got out of his car and, in the distance he could see a stunning view of The Chateau Cenevieres. A pretty French woman of around 35 years of age came out of one of the rear doors. Behind her, stood a boy of around 7 years of age and a girl of around 5 years of age.

"Jeux peux aidez vous?"

"Parlez vous anglaise", said Quinn.

"Of course."

"I'm an old friend of Francois', we used to live near each other in Ireland as kids. He said if ever I was this way, I should look him up."

She smiled,

"He will be so surprised. I've never met any of Francois' old friends. Please come in."

"Can I get you a drink?"

"If you have one, a beer would be nice."

They went inside and from the fridge she handed Quinn a bottle of cold Stella Artois.

"My name's Prudence."

Quinn shook her petite hand, "I'm Michael," he smiled

"So, Michael, you knew each other at school?"

"Well, not at school, but soon after as teenagers."

"What was he like back then?"

"Lively, always in trouble."

He diverted the conversation.

"Is that Lego?" He said to the young boy.

"I used to play with that when I was your age."

Lost in France April 1999

"I'm sorry he doesn't understand you. Francois isn't interested in teaching him to speak English."

Quinn got down on his knees and started playing with the boy. After around five minutes, the sound of a van pulled up into the courtyard. Bufee got out and slammed the door, looking at Quinn's' hire car with suspicion. As he came in, Quinn could see the look on his face was not one of joy. He stared down at Quinn on his knees with his little son. His wife spoke to him in English.

"Francois, your friend Michael is here."

Bufee looked at Quinn.

His wife could see something was wrong.

"Everything ok Francois?"

"Yes fine. I'll just take yah man into the front room, keep the kids in here, will you?"

Bufee closed the sliding wooden door to his front room and turned to Quinn.

"I know who you really are, what the fock are you doing here?" He said, in a quiet voice, trying to contain his anger.

"I want to talk to you about Jacob Candy."

"Why the fock should I tell you anything?"

"Well, I'm sure you don't want all your old mates, (especially the ones released by the Good Friday Agreement), to know where you now live. Not to mention the wife and three kids you abandoned back in Belfast."

You bastard. You wouldn't?"

"Wouldn't I?" Must say, it looks like you're doing alright for yourself these days, be a shame to lose it all."

Bufee sat down. He was knocking 50 years old and had built himself a new life working as a carpenter. Quinn assumed Bufee would think he was still in the British Army. He took out a packet of cigarettes from his shirt breast pocket and lit one. He was sitting in front of a large picture window overlooking a field of sunflowers. In the middle of the field a large hose was rotating, watering the crops.

"If I tell you, I want your guarantee there's no comebacks."

"No comebacks, I just want to get to the truth and then deal with Candy."

Bufee was still hesitant, he looked down at the floor and began to speak.

Lost in France April 1999

"Back in the eighties, I was buying arms for the UDA and I get to meet this flash bastard, who introduced himself as Simon Davis, a Brit Sergeant who says that his unit is confiscating loads of weapons and he can divert them to us, as long as the money is right. We agreed a deal, and all goes well for about a year. Then a large delivery doesn't turn up, so we decide to finish with him, in fact we were also going to finish him off, but your man insists we meet to put things right. So, I turn up at a pub just over the border in Dundalk and he's brought along a guy who's his commanding officer, non-other than Candy. Well of course, we think it's a set up, but after putting out some traps that they pass with flying colours, the arms keep coming. However, Candy now has a problem. He no longer needs Davis, so he sets up a raid in Londonderry and bang, Davis is gone. A guy in the house gets shot, Candy then gets wind that you know what's really happened from that fockin' drunk Hammond. The trouble was, Hammond was paranoid, so he actually tells Candy he's told you about the raid. It was Candy that arranged to have you hit in the pub.

He was well aware I knew what he'd been up to and that I'm not someone who wouldn't leave word of his little sideline if something happened to me, so there's no way he was doing a "Davis" on me that's for sure, so he offers me a new life in France, by telling the authorities that I've been informing for him and my life was now in danger. I left at the drop of a hat and it suited me for people to believe I'd been murdered."

Bufee lit another cigarette. Quinn could see he was uncomfortable talking like this.

"Did no one raise any concerns?"

"Nah, it was easy, and I'd had enough anyway."

"One other question. Do you know anything about the death of a journalist called Patrick Priestly around ten years ago?"

"Not much, but I do know he was asking questions about the shooting in that house with Candy and Davis, so it was very convenient that he took flight out of a seventh story window. There is always another willing Davis to do Candy's dirty work."

There was a silence, Bufee looked up,

"We all done?"

"Frankie, you've been very helpful."

Buffee looked up with pleading eyes.

"Tell me I'm safe."

Lost in France April 1999

"Don't see why not."

Quinn knew only too well, that if he was able to get to Bufee, someone like Candy could too. He opened the lounge door. His wife was standing in front of the cooker and the children were still playing. She turned to Bufee,

"Everything OK Francois?"

He nodded. As Quinn got into his car, Bufee appeared in the doorway, walked out to Quinn, who opened his window and Bufee leant in.

"Do you know how my kids are?"

"Sorry I don't."

"They'd be early twenties by now, I'd like to see them."

"Maybe you might want to resurrect yourself one Easter!"

"Fock off."

"See yah, Frankie."

Quinn reversed his car onto the track and headed back towards Toulouse.

CHAPTER TWELVE

Breaking Glass

The plane touched down at Gatwick at 8.30 pm. Quinn was tired. After ten years of not going near an airport, he was seeing a lot of aeroplanes lately.

As he came through passport control, that horrible feeling came over him, Quinn was panicking. He made his way to the men's toilet and closing the door, sat down in a cubicle, clasping his hands to his face, breathing heavily. After around five minutes, he started to calm down and as he did, he heard the main door swing open and footsteps approaching one of the urinals. A mobile phone went off.

"Yes, yes, I lost Quinn when I got held up at passport control. I know where he's parked, I'm gonna wait there." It was an English accent.

Whoever it was, Quinn was not going back to his car. *How long had they been following him and who were they?*

He made his way out of departures, walking quickly towards the pedestrian bridge and the lift that led to the bus parking. As he approached one of the stops, the Gatwick Express bus arrived. Quinn got on, paid and sat down. No one seemed to be following, but as the bus pulled away a male around thirty years of age ran alongside, but the driver ignored him. He had no luggage in his hand, so Quinn guessed it was one of Candy's men. An hour later the bus arrived outside Victoria Station. Quinn went inside the station and took several routes to lose anyone that might be following him.

He came out of a side entrance and jogged along Eccleston Street and checked in a two-star hotel called Hotel Ramada.

He got up to the room that although basic was clean and the room was a decent size. Quinn started to flick through the TV channels, and before long, fell asleep fully clothed and exhausted.

The next morning, he awoke at 6.30am, with the noise of groaning and a banging head board hitting the wall adjoining his. Quinn felt like he was sleeping in a knocking shop. After about five minutes, the banging stopped. Quinn showered from a showerhead that had the power of a watering can and went down for a breakfast that tasted of nothing. The dining room was empty apart from a big blonde man of around thirty years of age sipping coffee. As

Quinn got in the lift to go back up to his room, blondie pushed into the lift.

"Sank you," he said, in a loud voice with an Eastern European accent.

As the door closed, his bear sized hands, locked around Quinn's neck, lifting him off the floor. Quinn gasped and kicked out, Blondie groaned, fell to his knees and released Quinn, and as held his nether regions, Quinn hit him as hard as he could.

"Fuck," Quinn screamed hurting his own hand in the process. Blondie fell back against the metal wall, but the blow from Quinn seemed to re-energise the big man. He caught Quinn with a blow that hit the side of his head, smashing him against one of the advertising frames that shattered. Blondie took another swing, missing Quinn, but leaving a dent in the side wall. Quinn head butted the monster and without logic, he just threw himself at him. The two men grappled but Blondie was too strong and pushed Quinn away like he was tossing a child. Quinn slammed helplessly against the control button of the lift. The voice from the lift announced,

"Sixth floor."

Now the attacker reached inside his jacket and pulled out a serrated machete style blade about two feet long. With two hands, Quinn grabbed the monster's wrist that was holding the weapon. The two men were now in a high stakes clinch, up against the lift doors. Suddenly they opened, and both men fell backwards with Quinn on top of the attacker. The blade fell to the ground, a chambermaid screamed as she saw it. Quinn scrambled to his feet and ran towards the stairs. The monster picked up the machete and followed. On the sixth-floor landing, Quinn pressed the steel bar on a black fire door and ran onto the roof. Down the centre of the roof was a tiled walkway, with glass lantern style sky lights looking down into each fifth-floor bathroom. Quinn ran along the walkway until he reached a large chimney stack and could go no further. He turned. There was an old, rusted bar laying at the base of the stack, Quinn picked it up and as he did, the fire door swung open, banging against the brick work. The big man stood there for a second catching his breath with the machete in his hand. His lips were red with blood. He gingerly made his way across the roof towards Quinn. He took a swing at Quinn, but Quinn caught him with a swipe on the back of the head with the rusted bar. Blondie toppled over squarely on his back on one of the skylights. For a moment it held him and then like thin ice on a pond, little cracks appeared and then multiplied into a glass web, and he was gone. There was a sound of crashing glass and a scream as he hit what sounded like the floor of the bathroom below. When Quinn looked down, the big man had in fact landed into an empty bath. Laying there, bloodied in a cheap suit, the attacker wriggled slightly, but was in obvious pain. The bathroom door opened and an overweight bald man in his fifties, wearing the tiniest of Y fronts, looked at his bath and then looked up at Quinn. "What the fuck happened."

Quinn looked at the guy, "Fucked if I know!"

At that moment a young guy in a suit, obviously staff, appeared next to Quinn and looking down at Blondie, said,

"Everything OK sir?"

"Just some bloke desperate for a bath," he said, tossing the bar to the floor.

The young man looked bemused at Quinn and then down into the bathroom. As Quinn reached the fire escape door, he could hear another shout.

"What sort of fuckin' hotel is this anyway?"

He went to his room, quickly packed and took the stairs to the reception and paid. He knew the only way they could have been found, was by tracking him.

In a small café opposite the hotel, he made a note of the important numbers from his phone, that he felt he would need. He then took out his sim card a slipped it into his wallet.

Quinn opened the call box door nearby and dialled one of the numbers on his list.

A female voice said, "Colonel Caine's office."

"Could I speak with the Colonel?"

"Who's speaking please?"

"Could you tell him it's Michael Quinn."

There was a delay on the line of around thirty seconds.

"Quinn, how are you, my friend?"

"CAN we meet sir, it's urgent."

"I'm leaving early for home today. Can you come out to Claygate for around 3pm?"

"Of course."

He gave Quinn his address.

Colonel Charles Caine had been for a period, Quinn's commanding officer and it was Caine he would regularly brief on activities in Ireland, both on and off the record.

They would meet at various locations around Southern Ireland.

Quinn hired a Volkswagen Golf and headed out of London, listening to Nick Lowe on the car cassette. He found Pond Lane where the colonel lived and pulled up to a set of black electric gates. You couldn't see through them, as sheet metal had been mounted to block out prying eyes. In gold letters across the upright railings of the gates, read "Four Oaks." On Either side were brick pillars mounted with statues of eagles. Quinn pressed the buzzer, a CCTV camera looked down at him, and as he got back in his car, the gates creaked open. He pulled up to a second set of gates that also opened for him. The colonel was obviously taking no chances with security. As he drove along the gravel driveway, he passed a red phone box which was half covered with a willow tree. A large cherry blossom stood in front of a smart Edwardian house. The colonel appeared at the front door.

"Quinn, my boy, it must be what, ten years?"

"Fourteen, actually."

He shook Quinn's hand. Let's go for a walk and then we'll come back for a cuppa."

"Happy to walk if you are Colonel."

Quinn opened the boot of the VW and put on a ski jacket and baseball cap. The Colonel was in light tweeds and could've passed for either a farmer or a tic tac man at the races.

The two men walked up a narrow path, the day was cold with a biting wind.

"Well, it's been a long time Michael, what's so urgent?"

Colonel, you are one of the few people I can trust, that's why I'm here. I believe Jacob Candy murdered an occupant of a house in Londonderry, along with Sergeant Davis, on the same night in 1989. There was also the death of a journalist called Priestley, which I believe could be connected with an investigation he was doing on Candy.

The Colonel stopped walking.

"These are very serious charges Quinn."

"I also believe Candy gave a group of Republican's false information on myself and Hammond. In effect, he is using this breakaway faction as a tool to do his own killing."

"You have proof of the killing, Quinn?"

"Two witnesses. An officer called Mark Taylor, and a Protestant arms dealer, who is now living in France under a false identity."

"Come on Quinn, evidence from Taylor will never stand up. I remember his case, poor wretch, the other sides defence will make him out to be a mad man, you know that. And as for your man in France, will he testify?"

"No sir."

"Well Quinn, you have a problem."

The Colonel leant on a fence facing a paddock. Four young horses slowly came over to him. He pulled a small apple from his coat and fed one from his open palm. The two men carried on walking.

"You're claiming Candy wants to keep what he did quiet, but there is another problem you have. Our ex-terrorist friends on both sides of the divide aren't too keen on investigations into sins of the past. The world doesn't realise just how many informers there were, giving information to us. Some of them are now heroes and politicians. They don't want the embarrassment. Files to be kept closed in the national interest, suits just about everybody.

It's hard to get the Candy's of this world to be held accountable, they're too protected. They know too much. The security services will back him. The reality is; no one cares that hundreds, if not thousands of ex-soldiers have been and will continue to be sectioned, dying well before their time. They're the ones that are being prosecuted for killings, not your Candy's. Is it right that soldiers are answerable for their actions when under the Good Friday agreement Loyalists and Catholic terrorists got letters of comfort, that they wouldn't be prosecuted?

"Colonel, with respect, soldiers cannot be treated the same as those killers. Natural justice would argue that we should, but a soldier must be held to a higher account. I agree the Good Friday Agreement was unfair, but if you're pragmatic, it brought peace. Not all killings by a soldier can be excused. That's why we investigate, to uphold the law. The rules of engagement have to be followed or we're just like them. A civil rights marcher tending an injured person shot by a paratrooper on Bloody Sunday, is not the same as a soldier shooting a terrorist running away who's just committed a murder. I will always be on the soldier's side as long as I can understand why they opened fire."

The colonel didn't speak. (It was clear the colonel did not share his view). The two men crossed a wooden bridge onto a dirt track, a group of birds fluttered out of some bushes.

A church steeple came into view which signalled they were heading back towards the colonel's house. He held a wooden gate open for Quinn, that lead back into his rear garden.

THE DERRY SPY

Quinn looked at the field they were standing by.

"What are you growing here Colonel?"

"Probably a conscience."

"You know Quinn, I can never see this Ireland thing being resolved. I remember being told by a colleague that as far back as 1972, Michael Carver, Britain's most senior officer secretly suggested in a report, that Britain should escape the commitment to the border. In effect, he was proposing a united Ireland. We are still there 25 years later, but what's the answer? We have a chunk of the population who consider themselves British, so you can't just abandon them."

The Protestants feel more British than you or I. Like any religion or nationality under siege, you become more committed to it. Everywhere you see "no surrender" daubed on buildings. Telling them they are going to be ruled by Dublin would be as alien as telling someone in London, they are now answerable to Paris and not Westminster."

A loud shot rang out, Quinn flinched and crouched down. The colonel laughed.

"Quinn it's the cannon in the field. It goes off periodically to frighten off the birds."

Breaking Glass

Quinn was embarrassed, he stood back up.

There was a second blast, but this time, the colonel was flung against the back wall of his house. A third shot sounded and the lamp above the back door exploded with the impact. The colonel lay in a rose flowerbed, his shoulder and arm covered in blood.

"Get in the house," he gasped.

"There's a shotgun in the cabinet in the corner of the kitchen, shells in the draw underneath."

Quinn ran into the kitchen through the back door and grabbed the gun. He broke open the old Rigby and loaded two shells, putting another six into his pocket. He ran through the front of the house and made for the area where the shots had come from. As he moved through the wood land, he could see a flash of blue belonging to his assailant. Quinn kept on running towards the shooter, he could hear the crackle of boots on fallen branches. The sound of what he recognised as a Land Rover starting and a door slamming came through the trees and then he saw it, an old white defender. Quinn drew his gun. The first shot clanged off the bodywork spraying it with pellets His second shot took out one of the back lights. The Land Rover slid out of the forest and onto a pathway and pulled away. Quinn ran back to find the colonel who was still conscious but gasping for air. Quinn immediately called the emergency services.

The ambulance and police arrived and to Quinn's relief, the paramedics told Quinn, the colonel was going to be OK. The police questioned Quinn as if the colonel was the target, but Quinn knew it was he that they were after. He saw no mileage in telling the police anything different.

CHAPTER THIRTEEN

Paperback writer, April 1999

The rain was falling heavily on the drive back to London. *How had they found him? Was he followed?* Quinn parked his car in the outer perimeter of Regents Park.

He walked quickly across the park, through the iron gates and onto Baker Street. He went to a mobile phone shop and bought another pay as you go sim card. He looked up the number of the journalist who'd contacted him six months before and dialled his number.

"Evening, David Best, Guardian newspaper."

"David, it's Michael Quinn, you called me a few months back. Can you meet me tonight at 7pm at Reubens restaurant in Baker Street?"

"A bit short notice, isn't it?"

"Do you want a story or not?"

"Yes of course, I'll be there."

To keep out of the rain, Quinn bought a ticket at the cinema on the corner of Baker and Paddington Street and watched the first 50 minutes of The Green Mile with Tom Hanks.

Reubens is one of the last of the famous Jewish restaurants left in London. As you walk in, a smiling picture of the film director, Michael Winner greets you. A young waiter with a skull cap approached Quinn,

"Have you a booking, sir?"

"Er, no, but I'm after a table for two."

The waiter looked around

"Follow me please."

The waiter walked him to the back of the busy restaurant, he sat down, ordering a beer and a jug of water. The restaurant was busy with regulars tucking into various traditional dishes. Five minutes later, Best arrived and was shown to Quinn's table.

Best was around 40 years of age and looked like he'd just been dug up. He had a sallow complexion and was passionately untidy. It was hard to believe that only a few years ago, this man had been a showbiz reporter for one on the tabloids. He looked every inch the exhausted hack reporter. He sat down and dramatically announced,

"We meet at last Mr Quinn."

"Please, call me Michael."

"What a rotten night, thankfully a cab dropped me right outside."

Best ordered a beer and then they both ordered salt beef sandwiches. He pulled out a small black dog-eared notebook from his pocket.

"Must admit, I was surprised to hear from you. You gave me quite the brush off when I called you last October. You ok if I take some notes?"

Quinn nodded with approval but asked a question of his own.

"You met with Hammond just before he was killed," said Quinn leaning back in his chair.

"Yes, we met at his house, in Suffolk. Drank like a bloody fish though. I staggered out of there half pissed."

"Did he discuss Jacob Candy?"

"I take it you're talking about the M.P. Jacob Candy?"

"Yes."

"No, I met him to talk about the Mountbatten case, which he worked on when he first arrived in Ireland."

"Why are you interested in the Mountbatten case? He was killed by the IRA."

Best took a greedy gulp of his beer and wiped his lips with the back of his hand.

"Well, there lies a story. Interestingly, the only person to be convicted of Mountbatten's murder was Thomas McMahon, an IRA bomber trained in Libya. He was jailed for life but let out under the Good Friday Agreement in 1998. Francis McGirl, a known activist for the provisional IRA was also arrested but acquitted. He died in 1995 when a tractor toppled on top of him, which is pretty suspicious, especially when you take into account that the SAS were said to be in the area at the time.

All the documents relating to the death of Mountbatten are closed, sighting national security. Mountbatten had been an IRA target since 1960 but the assassination had been vetoed by the IRA's chief of staff. In spite of warnings, he kept going to Ireland every year. He always claimed the Irish were his friends and that he felt safe. In 1979 when he was killed, it was the first year the boat wasn't searched before he boarded. Although intelligence sources claim McGuiness ordered the attack, but did the IRA actually do it?"

Paperback writer, April 1999

"This is all news to me!"

"It gets worse."

An Irish criminal called Patrick Holland who was planning a book about the assassination, saying Mountbatten had been killed by the British Security forces because he knew secrets about the Royal Family that could harm them. Mountbatten also held certain controversial political views and was saying quite a bit to journalists about his colourful private life the year before his death. Holland was found dead in his cell aged 70. The Irish Garda has never closed the file on Mountbatten, as they believe there was a wider conspiracy, so it's still an active case. It has been deemed politically expedient not to pursue inquiries. If the IRA did kill him, it was a big own goal. There was a public outcry and funding from the US dried up after the killing. Mountbatten had been sympathetic to Republican aims and had offered himself as a middleman negotiator."

"You truly believe all that conspiracy stuff?"

"Look, two years ago, Diana Spencer dies in an underpass in Paris. Now who the fuck dies in an empty underpass in Paris at three in the morning? I don't buy it, very convenient and let's face it, she was seen as a potential threat to the Royals and the establishment. Now I don't think for one minute, members of the Royal Family are going around ordering assassinations, but do I believe factions who have got the Royals interests at heart think, it's their role, to carry out such acts."

Quinn gave Best a doubtful look. The food arrived, Best continued eating and talking at the same time.

"Think about it Quinn. We have right-wing so-called think tanks in this country, who not only have politicians amongst their ranks, but some very dangerous individuals. Say within a group, there's some extremists, who want this country to be run in a certain way and will stop at nothing, and I mean nothing. It's not as mad as it sounds. Do you ever wonder why so many people that have gone off script end up dead? The situation in this country is not dissimilar to the Illuminati in the US. Kennedy goes against the National Rifle Association and the generals and not only is he shot by a lone gun man, but the lone gun man is killed on the way to court by a guy who only had six months to live, so the secrets died with him very quickly. Kennedy's brother Bobby also gets assassinated by a lone gun man. Apart from Regan who got shot but survived, all other presidents that tow the line with the establishment, have lived a long happy life. You might get different governments, but basically, it's always the same people in charge. There's a great cartoon of Bill Clinton after he'd been in office for about a year. He's sitting in the Oval Office and leaning back on his chair, with his feet on his desk, talking to his team, with the caption saying, "Here's what I'd do if I was President." It's the same in this country Quinn, nothing changes. We are here talking because your friend Hammond's dead. Can it be a coincidence, that within a week of seeing him, my flat gets turned over? We know the entire security community are under pressure from certain factions, and I'm not talking about just politicians. It's the wealthy, the bankers, powerful families, rich industrialists and newspaper proprietors funding all those fuckin' weird organisations. They want you to see the world as they see it and if you don't, well woe betide you. The status quo has to be maintained as it has been for years and years and I'm sorry, but they won't stand for anyone rocking the boat."

Quinn ordered another two beers. In a quiet voice, he then set out to Davis his accusations regarding Candy.

"Fuckin' hell Michael, this is great stuff and you're telling me you don't believe in conspiracies?"

He scribbled down in his notebook frantically.

Quinn leant forward,

"I think Candy panicked because he thought Hammond had spilt the beans on him, what do you know about Candy?" Said Quinn.

"Well, he got handed a nice safe seat in the last election. Rising star in the party, gets his money from the family property business. It operates from offices on the fourth floor of Millbank Tower, where conveniently, Conservative Party HQ is. So, he's nice and close to do a bit of lobbying and of course, he now has higher political ambitions and lots of powerful friends. Lives in a penthouse apartment in Kensington, married to an ex-Miss South Africa. He's certainly climbing the greasy political pole."

"Any scandals?"

"Not that I'm aware of, but let me do some digging, and I will come back to you. Now, what about an interview then, for my piece on Mountbatten?"

Next time David, let's see if we can get Jacob Candy nailed first. I think there's plenty there for a start."

Best finished off his beer putting his notebook into a scruffy satchel.

"I will ring his office tomorrow and try and get a statement from Candy."

"Well, the shit will really hit the fan, if you contact him direct."

Paperback writer, April 1999

Quinn paid the bill.

"Do be careful Best."

They both left the restaurant.

Quinn picked his car up and moved it near his hotel at Rutland Gate. On the corner was a phone box and he decided to ring home. His brother answered the phone.

"Mike, you ok? We've been trying to reach you, but your phone's always off."

"It's been off as it was being tracked."

"Fuckin hell Michael! Anyway, a guy called the house today and mum spoke to him. He asked for you and said you'd know him as JK."

James Klein, known as JK was an ex-colleague of Quinn's in Germany and had been one of his contacts in Ireland. Quinn guessed he'd used the JK pseudonym as he would have been worried Quinn's family home phone was being tapped.

"Did he leave a number?"

No, but mum has left a message, hang on, I'm trying to read her writing. She told him she thought you were in

London. He said if you were, he could meet at 9pm outside your old haunt where you used to meet. He said he'd wait there for fifteen minutes. Does that mean anything?

"Yes thanks, Tom. Listen, I will keep in touch."

"Look after yourself Michael."

Quinn put the phone down, he checked his watch, he had half an hour to get to where they used to meet up.

He walked hurriedly to South Kensington Station. On the way, he thought about Klein. In Northern Ireland Klein was viewed as a bit too righteous to some. Years before, Quinn and Klein would meet up on leave before they were both posted to Ireland, at a Polish restaurant called The Daquish. They'd got on well, Klein was from a fairly religious Jewish family of Polish descent, so like Quinn, he wasn't part of the old schoolboy network. The Daquish was discreet and an unlikely location to find two young officers.

He arrived outside the restaurant just before 9pm. After around five minutes a woman of around 30 years of age came up to him.

"I'm with James Klein. Look as if you're giving me directions, in case we are being watched, he wants you to get in the cab that's parked across the road, reg K493 JGL He's driving."

Still play acting, she smiled, thanked him and carried on walking. Quinn walked across the road and got in the back of the cab. The amber light on top switched off.

"Sorry for the cloak and dagger Quinn, but you're almost certainly being tailed, and this is probably the only way we can talk under their noses without them knowing we've met. Fortunately, my brother-law's a cabbie, so he lent me this!"

Quinn could see Klein's face in the rear-view mirror. He'd aged a lot since they'd last met. His once black hair was now silver but he still looked a tough cookie.

"I heard what happened to you at your place in Appethorpe. They want us gone Quinn, because of what we know about the murder of Davis and their operation with Candy."

"Klein, what operation?"

"You really don't know, do you?

In February of 1990, an informer told army intelligence that Candy was selling confiscated arms to the loyalists. He was pulled in and after a series of interviews the decision was made, that he was involved so deep with the loyalists, rather than charge him, the army could use him. For the next three years, he fed us intelligence details on their operations and personnel. Where guns were hid, their targets, everything. He was very useful. I had to be careful dealing with him, because he was such a slippery bastard. I was his handler.

After a few months, the same source comes to me and says that Candy killed Davis, as well as an Irishman called Brady in a house in Londonderry the previous Christmas. So firstly, I pulled Hammond in for an interview to the Penthouse in Belfast, it's what we called the top floor of the Dibbis flats that overlooked the Falls and Shanklin Road areas. The only way in or out, was by helicopter. So, I get him flown in and he can't stop talking. I then pull Candy in and of course, he denies everything, but I knew he was a guilty as hell. Problem was, Candy is now such an asset to us, we're stuck. Hammond with our encouragement quietly left the army, as we were worried, he'd expose Candy."

"So, you get an officer like Hammond to resign to protect a killer?

"Quinn, those as you know, were difficult times. It was a means to a justifiable end. Hammond was a piss head anyway; he wouldn't have lasted much longer in the army."

Paperback writer, April 1999

Klein stopped the cab along Exhibition way and turned in his seat and looking at Quinn, said,

"So, five years on and to me it's all ancient history, as I left the army in 1994. Then four weeks ago, a car just misses me in a small road where I live, which I put down to just some idiot's driving. Then two days later, I'm at Earls Court tube station and as the train comes in, a monster of a man slams into me, but luckily a young guy grabs my arm, or I'd be a gonna. I then read about Hammond, and I hear through the grapevine about you. Quinn I've been doing a bit of digging on Candy and we aren't just dealing with some rogue soldier, covering up what a naughty boy he's been, we're up against something much bigger. He's being lined up into a senior position in government to work in the interests of some dangerous people. He is very important to them, I believe, the only way we will be safe is for him to be out of the picture."

"You mean kill him?"

"Well, if this was Ireland and we had to take out a terrorist, we'd plan it with no qualms."

Quinn looked out of the cab window and back at Klein."

"I tell you what Klein, you're fuckin mad. You just can't go around killing people and think you can get away with it."

"Quinn, what do you think the British government have been doing in Ireland for the past forty years? Wakeup, won't you?"

"Sorry Klein, it's not for me. Don't tell me anymore, we'll forget we ever had this conversation."

Klein passed Quinn a card.

"This is a number for me, which I will keep switched on. If you're in trouble or change your mind, ring me."

"I appreciate that. Good to see you JK, sorry I can't be of help."

Quinn got out, but before Klein pulled away, he opened the passenger window and called to Quinn,

"Be careful my friend."

Quinn caught the train from South Kensington to Green Park. There's a long tunnel that connects the Jubilee to the Piccadilly line. He waited at the top of the tunnel and looking back, waiting for the train to pull in. He ran down the steps, and made it onto the train, just as the doors closed.

After getting off at Victoria, he walked back to his car, taking his bag from the boot. He passed the Russian Orthodox Cathedral in Ennismore Gardens and spotted the Imperial Hotel and checked into what the receptionist described as their last deluxe room available. Quinn went up to his room, which seemed to have been styled on an East German apartment from the 1970's. The receptionist's description was obviously off a script for foreign visitors. If a Stasi agent had appeared from a wardrobe, he wouldn't have been surprised. Spartan would be an understatement. Quinn went down to the lobby, where there was an old phone booth with a wooden concertina door. The glass windows had obviously been knocked out long ago. He rang Best.

"Quinn, I'm glad you've rung. A friend at one of the red tops has been having Candy followed by a private detective for a potential story. I've got some interesting stuff on him. By the way, I've just spoken to his office for a word on the deaths of Brady, Taylor and Davis. Got the usual "no comment."

"Hang on, you said, Taylor?"

"Sorry, I thought you would have known, he was found dead this afternoon, he was strangled."

Quinn felt dizzy, his legs went beneath him and he perched on the little seat inside the booth. He'd given Taylor's name to Brady, thinking her people would not touch such a damaged man. *Had he led them to him?*

He stumbled over his words. "Can you meet me at my hotel.?"

An hour later Best, was sitting opposite him. He reached into his satchel and took out an A4 envelope. There's plenty in there Quinn, including photographs."

Quinn flicked through the contents of the envelope.

"This is good, thank you."

Best looked around, he was nervous, and Quinn was solemn and not talking much.

"Quinn, the guy that gave me this is usually fearless. When I asked him about Candy, he said that they weren't running any story, but if I decided to, be it on my head. They're obviously shit scared!"

It was the first time Best had seemed nervous.

Quinn put his drink down and said,

"Don't worry, no one else will see this."

Best stood up,

"I'm really sorry about your friend, I betta go."

Another hour passed and the bar was busy with mainly elderly tourists. Quinn sat there, drinking scotch after scotch, getting drunker by the minute, thinking about Taylor and what Klein had said to him about assassinating Candy. The unthinkable had become the thinkable. *Why would they kill Taylor? Hadn't the poor bastard suffered enough?*

The barman looked at his empty glass.

"Another, for you sir?"

"Why not?"

A woman of around 35 years of age, with a large cleavage on show, in a short mini dress approached him.

"Fancy some company love?"

"I appreciate the offer, but I wouldn't be a lot of good to you tonight, but thankyou anyway."

"Well, at least it's a polite turn down," she smiled and remained on the bar stool next to him.

Quinn started to well up, he felt completely overwhelmed.

"Are you ok?" asked the woman he'd just spoken to.

Quinn said nothing and wiped his eyes with the back of his hands. She sat next to him and put a motherly arm around him."

"Bad news love?"

"An old friend."

"Well, if you need comforting, if you know what I mean, I'll be over there. Might even give you a discount!"

She took a position further along the bar.

He sat drinking and watched her get picked up by a "client" about ten minutes later.

"We're closing now sir," said the barman apologetically.

Quinn looked at his watch, it was 1am. He moved slowly towards the lift. On reaching his room he fumbled the key in his room door and in the darkness climbed onto the bed, drunk.

CHAPTER FOURTEEN

Mcloed Road

At 6am the crashing sound of empty bottles being wheeled out in a huge bin, woke Quinn. He felt terrible and he immediately thought of Taylor. *Just another loose end tidied up?*

As Quinn focussed in the darkness, sitting on a chair was an outline of something or someone. Quinn startled, sat up and switched on the bedside lamp, which illuminated her face.

What the.." It was Brady.

"Now, now, Michael, this is your lucky day."

"You and the word lucky don't go together."

"They've sent me to finish the job on you, but as you know, the person I want, is Jacob Candy, but I need your help.

By the way you look like shite."

"It was a bad night."

"Well, if I were you, I'd be more careful. I told them at reception I was your sister and they let me into your room. I coulda finished you off in your sleep. For an ex- spy you're not very good are yah?"

He slowly moved his legs round, got up and held his hand to his head as he stumbled to the bathroom. Brady made him a black coffee.

Quinn showered and dressed into the same clothes he'd been wearing the day before. He needed to buy some more clothing, but that would have to wait until later.

He stood in the doorway of the bathroom and looked at Brady, sitting in a chair with her feet up on the end of the bed, drinking tea, reading the contents of the envelope Best had given Quinn."

Did you kill Taylor?"

"Who the fock is Taylor?"

"The same Taylor, I told you of, the one in a mental home."

"Oh him. I don't deny I hate you lot, but I'm not into killing cripples. Changing the subject, we need to move quickly on Candy as my people are getting itchy about what I'm up to."

Quinn leant against the door frame and just stared at her.

She got up and wrote an address on some hotel note paper.

"Can you meet me at this address at 11am, It's an old IRA safe house near Woolwich. No one else apart from a lady called Sharon and me will be there. I'm trusting you, so don't pull any strokes!"

Quinn looked at the address.

"I'll be there. By the way, how did you find me?"

Picking up Best's envelope she turned to Quinn, "Danny Boy sent us your whereabouts."

"Can I borrow this?"

"Be my guest, but I'd like it back later, as I told the owner, no one else would see it."

"Naughty."

After she'd left, Quinn went back to the call box in the lobby and dialled Klein's number.

"Klein, it's Quinn."

"How yah doing," said Klein.

"Have you heard about Taylor?"

"Yes."

"How did you find out?"

"Quinn, you know how it is, there's always someone in the services who owes you one."

"I thought about what you said and I'm in."

"Well, that's great!"

"But first, I want you to meet someone. Do you know where the seaman's memorial is?"

"Yes, of course."

"Meet me there at ten this morning."

Quinn left his hotel; he'd decided he needed to bring Klein to meet Brady. He went into a busy café, full of the young and upwardly mobile, who the press had labelled Sloane Rangers. Some of the girls were dressed as Diana Spencer lookalikes even though she'd now been gone some two years. He ordered a coffee and sat facing the door. No one obvious came in that he thought could be following him, but he was taking no chances. He paid the bill and asked to use the gents and as he approached them, he could see a rear entrance leading onto a narrow street. He left through it and ran about a hundred yards, turning at a right angle onto The Kings Road, which he crossed, and darted into a news agents. He picked up a magazine, pretending to browse through it. Running out of an alleyway, came a thick set male in a wax jacket, (no doubt to make him fit in with the locals). He stopped and looked both ways and retrieved a mobile phone from his jacket. A double decker bus stopped outside where Quinn was, blocking the view, he boarded it, leaving his pursuer standing there with hands on hips.

Quinn got off at Sloane Square and walked onto the station concourse and up three small flights of stairs. After less than a minute the train that goes all the way to Upminster on the District line arrived. Quinn sat down; it was busy. There was a group of young twenty something girls, standing and laughing but also trying to outshout each other in their estuary drawl.

As the train pulled into Temple, an announcement of "mind the gap" sounded. As the doors were about to close, Quinn quickly rose and stepped onto the platform. Temple is one of the quietest stops on the District Line. No one else appeared, so he was confident that he was not now being followed. He caught the next train to Tower Hill station and walked straight past the food wagon that he remembered from his school days and entered the memorial gardens, a circular area in remembrance of merchant seamen who have died in both world wars. The area stands in the shadow of the former Port of London Authority Head Quarters, 10 Trinity Square. As he walked towards the covered mausoleum like structure that faces the Thames, the girl he'd seen the day before approached him. She smiled and as she passed him said,

"Just by the gate, he's waiting for you."

Quinn found the black cab waiting on the cobbled street.

"Who's the girl?"

"That's my daughter, she's worried about me and wants to help."

Quinn nodded with approval.

"Right, where we off to?" Klein asked, clicking on his seat belt.

"I want you to come and meet a woman called Helen Brady."

Klein turned in his seat.

"You're fuckin' mad. I saw her being questioned in Belfast by the RUC some years ago, she's a fuckin nut job."

"She may be, but she's also the daughter of Derek Brady who Candy murdered, and she wants him more than we do. She's at a safe house in Woolwich and wants to meet."

"Fuckin' great. Two ex-army off to the lion's den. Have you lost your mind?"

You got a better idea? She's up for taking Candy out, that's all we want. After that, who cares."

Klein thought for a moment and said, "It's your call Quinn, but I don't like it one bit."

They travelled along the A13 and then through The Blackwall Tunnel, heading towards Woolwich and onto Abbey Wood.

Mcleod Road, Abbey Wood, is an unusually long road of small, terraced houses. It is in what was the heart of the Irish community in South London, from the 1950's to the early1980's. The workers used to get the little pedestrian ferry from Erith nearby, to take them across the Thames, to the Dagenham Ford Motor Plant. It was an area Quinn knew well, because as a kid, everybody seemed to have an Irish relative that lived in this road. The irony that the IRA operated a safe house here, wasn't lost on Quinn.

The property looked like the typical home of an elderly resident, long grass in the front garden, that reached turquoise woodwork last painted in the 1960's.

Quinn tapped on the front door, hanging from which, was a remnant of a bell long gone.

After about thirty seconds, a short masculine woman with dyed blonde hair, opened the front door.

In a broad Irish accent she said, "Hello lads, come in." *(This must be Sharon*, thought Quinn).

Klein pulled a puzzled face at Quinn.

She stood back to let them into the hallway and closed the front door. Brady immediately appeared from the kitchen. Quinn introduced Klein. She was dressed in a black turtleneck, black jeans and flat boots. She looked every inch the action woman and very attractive.

"Helen Brady meet ex-captain, James Klein."

"You never told me you'd have company." She said.

"You can trust him." Said Quinn.

Klein just stared at her.

Mcloed Road

"Follow me," said Brady. They went into a small morning room where she rolled back a rug which revealed a small door, set in the floor, which she pulled open. There was a small flight of steps leading into a basement.

"The IRA dug this out in the 1970's. It leads into the back garden, and you can leave, via an alley out of the back."

Quinn and Klein followed her cautiously into the basement. "Sharon" closed the door above them. They were in a room around eight feet wide and twenty foot long. There was a small kitchen, a bathroom and a table in the middle of the room.

"Thought it best to meet here in case you're being followed. You can't get a phone signal down here which is a plus, if someone's tracking you. Anyone for tea or coffee?"

Klein spoke for the first time.

"Coffee for me."

Quinn took his jacket off and said,

"Same for me."

He stood at at the table as did Klein. On it were two pictures, a map of central London and four pages of type written observations regarding Candy. These were all from the envelope Brady had taken from Quinn.

She placed three coffees on the table, and she began.

"I've studied the contents of the envelope on Candy. He's well-guarded most of the time, but there is a weakness. On Monday nights he comes back to London, I'm guessing he tells his wife he needs to be in town to get ready for the upcoming week. He attends a meeting at Millbank and then at 6pm on the dot, his driver picks him up in a black S Class Mercedes. He gets dropped off at his girlfriend's place. Her name's Victoria Rogers, pictured here." She tapped the picture in front of him. The picture was of a pretty woman, nudging forty years of age. Brady continued.

"Quite a high-flying solicitor. She lives in a flat in Mayfair. We need to get to her before Candy arrives, and that's where we need two of us at her flat and a third person following Candy."

She looked at Klein,

"Lucky you turned up Klein, you up for it?"

He nodded.

"What do you want me to do?"

"I need you to follow Candy from Millbank and text me and Quinn as he makes his way to her. We need to know when he's outside. Once there, your jobs done, just disappear."

"When Candy arrives, I will give him his last rights."

Klein nodded in approval at Brady's suggestion. He leant back against the cellar wall.

"How can you be sure Rogers will open your door to you?"

Brady smiled. "Who wouldn't open the door to a poor nun?"

Quinn remembered these had been the exact words of Shamus just before he got killed in Dublin.

"What about Rogers?"

"We will tie her up or something. Don't worry we aren't going to do anything nasty."

Brady ran her forefinger along the map on the table. I've marked the route from Candy's office to her flat in Cork Street. I suggest we do it tomorrow night."

Both Quinn and Klein silently nodded to acknowledge Brady's urgency to get on with it.

Quinn took a sip of black coffee and pointing to the map said,

"What about weapons?" Said Klein

"You won't need one. I'll be armed and Quinn, can you get a gun, just in case?"

Quinn thought for a second.

"I should be able to."

Brady got up and opened the top draw of a wooden filing cabinet. She took out a Glock pistol. She then reached back in the draw and retrieved a silencer with a box of ammunition. She put both in a rucksack, out of which she pulled out a balaclava and some gloves and threw them to Quinn.

"You'll need these."

He looked at the wool mask with two eye holes and a mouth hole.

"You'll look like fuckin' provo," remarked Klein.

"You should be so lucky," retorted Brady.

From the same rucksack, she took out a mobile phone and passed it to Klein.

"Take this phone and just before 6pm tomorrow, switch it on. Follow Candy once he gets picked up and text us as to where he is. Inside the envelope is a number for the phone we have. Throw the phone when the job is done. Got it?"

Klein obediently nodded and placed the phone in his jacket pocket. Brady looked at Quinn.

"You good to meet outside her flat just before 5pm tomorrow, or as you boys would say, nineteen hundred hours."

"It's seventeen hundred hours actually," said Klein, correcting her. "

"Whatever."

Quinn gathered up the contents of the envelope. He admired her organisational skills and liked the plan.

"Same way out?" Said Klein.

"No, you will need to follow me", said Brady.

She opened a steel door at the end of the room. She switched on a torch and the three of them crouched and made their way along a damp cold tunnel, which was around sixty feet long. It was held up with wooden rafters, like a scene from an old prisoner of war film. They came to a set of steps and Brady shined a light onto a door above them.

"Just push and you'll come up into a garden shed and then out into an alleyway."

"See you tomorrow then," said Quinn.

"Tomorrow it is." She gave Quinn a mock salute.

Klein didn't even acknowledge Brady, he simply followed Quinn up into the shed. Five minutes later they were in Klein's cab driving along the Woolwich Road. Klein looked at Quinn through his rear-view mirror.

"It's a solid plan but she worries me."

"She'll come good James," said Quinn

"She's still a fuckin' psycho as far as I'm concerned."

"Well, we've both known a few."

Klein dropped Quinn off in Piccadilly, just outside Cordings, the famous old menswear outfitters. He made his way passed a green wooden news stand down into the tube station. It was a Sunday afternoon, so the station was quiet. He kept looking around. He came back out though the entrance that leads to Leicester Square and hailed a cab back to the hotel, where he knew he was vulnerable, but gambled that Candy's team (whoever they were), were waiting on Brady to deal with him, not knowing she had her own agenda. The bar of the hotel was quiet, most of the guests had gone home, as Sunday was a popular change over day.

What would tomorrow bring? After all he was doing a deal with the devil, in the form of Helen Brady.

"Scotch?" said the barman.

"Why not?" Said Quinn with a smile. *I must cut down the booze after this is over,* thought Quinn

Quinn sat in the lounge bar, and it gradually filled up with arriving guests.

He was nervous. This was always the worst time, waiting for the start an operation, but this was no ordinary job. Would they be caught? Would they even get to Jacob Candy?

It was midnight when he arrived back in his room. He didn't sleep much. He listened to the sirens, the deliveries, showers being run, the air conditioning switching on and off. At 6am Quinn sat in the dark going through the plan in his mind, over and over. He got up, dressed smartly in blue slacks, white shirt and a blue jumper. He looked like he could be going for a game of golf rather than a kill. He sat there, breathing heavily. He packed his clothes into his holdall.

At 7am, he left the hotel. At the bus stops, queues of cleaners and early shift workers waited for the buses and delivery vans stopped and started.

He reached his hired car and placed his belongings in the boot. He walked to Hyde Park and as he got there, daybreak brought the birdsong. He'd always loved dawn in London. He could hear the sound of the wind rustling the trees in Hyde Park. The joggers listening to their Wartman's outnumbered the swans and the ducks. A dog walker approached him with a jolly "Good morning." Quinn forced a smile. He sat on a bench that was dedicated to a Nancy Wright, with the inscription, "*Her Favourite Place.*" He thought about his life, which if he was honest, hadn't reached his expectations.

The "Café on the Lake" opened and Quinn was their first customer. He ordered a tea and as he gazed out, in the water he spotted a swimmer, with her dog swimming beside her. It was quite an amazing spectacle of loyalty. *She must be mad, it's freezing*, he thought.

It was now 9.30am, he finished a cold coffee, paid the girl at the counter and started walking back. Thoughts of friends long gone, some alive, some dead, went through his mind. All those lives lost. *Was it really worth it?*

He moved out of the way of a horse and rider trotting along the park bridal way. The multicoloured hire boats on the lake were moored up together like a colourful honeycomb. It was now 11am.

He arrived back at his hotel and checked out. As he crossed the road looking left and right, he spotted a woman looking at him. She was casually dressed, around twenty-five years of age, he instinctively knew it was a tail, *inexperienced,* he thought, *far too obvious.*

He walked along Brompton Road and stopped and looked in the reflection of a book shop's window, he could see the woman, she stopped and turned to look in a clothing shop. He crossed the now busy road and made for one of the double door entrances of Harrods. Two burley security men, one Asian, were watching the entrance.

"Listen guys, I'm looking for a woman who's just stolen from my shop."

He described the girl in detail. The Asian guard said,

"We've seen no one like that sir."

"Ok no problem, I'll keep looking for her."

As Quinn cut through to the perfume department, he looked back to see the two security guards stopping the woman. He headed out to the side door and down the steps into Kensington High Street station.

He reached the ticket office, looked around and ran up the stairs coming out at street level. Quinn raised his arm.

"Where to mate?"

"Can you take me to Wildings Guns, Pimlico?"

"No problem."

Quinn jumped in the cab and as he passed the main doors at Harrods, he could see his tail still arguing with the two security men.

CHAPTER FIFTEEN

Danny Boy

Pimlico is an area of London neighbouring Chelsea, with some streets formed of nineteenth century houses. For years it has been an area popular with the hunting and shooting set. It was a clever move for ex-Major George Wilding, quartermaster to the British Army to open his gunsmiths shop here in 1986. He'd had a distinguished career, an expert in guns and it was this common interest had brought him and Quinn together during Quinn's training in Scotland with the A14.

The cab turned into Clarendon Street. No 15 was a classic Edwardian shop, double fronted, with a marble sign facia of gold on black, reading "Wilding and Sons." He pressed the buzzer and through the glass at one of the counters he could see Wilding. The lock clicked open, and Quinn entered and a young man he guessed was one of Wilding's sons, was at another counter trying to sell a restored vintage shot gun to a client. Wilding was in his late sixties, around 6ft 2 "tall, slightly stooped. He had a full head of grey hair, swept back. He was in shooting wear, looking like he should be out on a moor somewhere.

"Fuck me, it's the mighty Quinn!" he Roared. (It was a nick name Quinn had acquired whilst training).

"It's a long time since I've heard that expression."

"Come into my magic kingdom!"

Wilding led him into a small scruffy office that had files and paperwork everywhere. He plonked himself in a worn captain's chair behind an old partner desk. Behind him was a discoloured portrait of the Queen dating from the 1950's.

"Do sit dear boy. Sorry about the mess, fucking cleaner left a few months back. Good to see you. When did you leave, 1980 was it?"

"79, been leading a quiet life."

Wilding sat back and looked at Quinn knowingly.

"Can't be that fucking quiet, as people only come and see me out of the blue when they've got trouble!"

Quinn recounted the attacks on him, the deaths of Taylor and Hammond, without mentioning what he was planning next.

Danny Boy

"So, you're looking for a gun to use for self-protection?"

Wilding smiled and lent forward. He opened a yellow box of King Edward cigars sitting on his desk and offered one to Quinn.

"Not for me thanks."

He took a while to light the cigar, puffing at it vigorously, blowing smoke in Quinn's direction.

"You will recall the favoured gun with The Det was The Browning HP, I have one here with no markings and no history. If you get caught with it, you say you brought it back from Ireland concealed when on leave years ago, you understand?"

"Yes."

"Under no circumstances can the gun be traced back to me. Don't make your problem my problem."

Wilding got up and took some books off a bookshelf. He opened a large shelled out Encyclopaedia.

Inside packed in foam was a Browning HP handgun with a silencer and ammunition.

"He placed it in front of Quinn.

"Yours for a mere thousand pounds."

Quinn picked the gun up and checked it.

"Rather expensive George."

"Buyers' market, dear boy!"

Quinn wasn't in a position to bargain. He took out an envelope and slid it onto the desk. Wilding didn't check it or touch it, he just left the money lying there, as if it was irrelevant. Quinn put the gun into his waistband. He slid the silencer into his inside pocket.

"You'll need these."

Wilding gave him a box of bullets.

He looked back at Wilding and said,

"Can I ask you a question, major?"

"Go ahead my boy."

"Why do it? Why take the risk and sell these "ghost" guns or whatever they're called?"

Wilding leaned back in his chair and took a long draw on his cigar and placed it in an ash tray, folded his arms and leant forward onto his desk.

"Do you know, after all those years in the army, how fucking boring it is, to sell beautiful weapons to some of these fuckin' hooray Henry's who haven't got a clue? So, if I can help an ex-comrade, and earn a few pounds and add a bit of excitement, why not? Just make sure that gun doesn't fuckin' come back to me. I will deny it anyway. Good luck and use it wisely."

He said it in a way, as if dismissing Quinn.

As Quinn left, the shop that was now empty of customers, he checked his watch, it was 2.05pm.

The walk to Bruton Street took just over half an hour. Again, he changed direction, going into shops, through escalators, in and out of hotels to shake off possible tails.

He went into the Coach and Horses pub, one of Mayfair's smallest pubs, he had no appetite, so ordered a Guinness, (which he nursed) and read the papers. It crossed his mind, *could this be his last time in a pub?* At 4.30, after three pints, he left and waited and watched the entrance to Rogers' apartment, from the top of Cork Street Mews.

At 4.55pm, he spotted Brady in full nun's outfit, crossing the road towards him. She certainly looked the part and had her small ruck sack in her hand. They met by the doors to Victoria Rogers' flat. He pressed the buzzer. They shared the same anticipation of what was about to happen. He could see their reflection in the glass doors of the entrance.

A voice came through the intercom.

"Hello, Victoria Rogers speaking."

"Oh, hello Victoria, It's Sister Mary from Saint Bernadette's Primary School, could I have a very quick word about a some help we need for the little ones?"

"I'm rather busy at the moment. Can you come back another time, sister?"

Brady looked at Quinn and shrugged.

"Sorry Victoria, but I'm going on retreat tomorrow, if you could give me just two minutes of your time, I'd be very grateful."

There was a delay of around twenty seconds that felt like an hour.

"Ok, but please make it quick."

There was a buzzing sound, then the outer door lock released. They climbed the stairs slowly and Quinn slipped the black balaclava over his face and put a pair of gloves on. Brady put on some latex gloves. As Victoria Rogers opened the door, Brady pulled out the silenced Glock 37 from her bag and said,

"Don't scream and don't panic, we're not going to hurt you." Quinn followed both women into a beautifully decorated lounge. Rogers had started to well up. She was wearing a short red dress, was made up heavily, like an air stewardess. She wore expensive jewellery and was slim with long blonde hair, she was frightened.

"Where's your phone? Said Brady sternly.

"On the table." She pointed to it.

"Is there a code?

"No."

Brady took from her bag cable ties and some gaffer tape and gave it to Quinn, who said,

"Victoria, I'm going to tie you up, that's all. I'm not going to hurt you."

The bedroom door was open, and he guided her into it. There was a large double bed with an iron bedstead at both ends.

"Lay on the bed." Said Quinn.

"What are you going to do to Jacob?"

At this point he lied.

"No harm will come to him. We just want to ask him some questions." As he applied the cable ties, not too tight, she started to cry again. As she lay there vulnerable, scared, he felt sorry for her. He put the tape over her mouth, whilst Brady watched from the doorway.

"I'm sorry, Victoria," said Quinn.

Brady was smirking, which Quinn found disturbing.

He closed the door and thankfully it blocked out the sound of her sobbing.

Quinn took off his balaclava, Brady took off her headdress.

It was now 5.15pm.

Quinn and Brady sat next to each other on the couch, like a couple on a bad date, not knowing what to say.

"Well, this is nice," said Quinn.

There followed a deathly silence apart from a clock ticking.

"You know Quinn, I kinda wish you and me had done the deed that night at the cottage."

"Should I be flattered you'd rather shag and then kill me rather than a straight execution?"

She smiled.

"As I told you at the time, you are one hell of an actress."

"Well I did study drama at uni."

"I'd say you wasted your talent."

It felt weird to Quinn but he did find her attractive. Another period of silence followed.

5.35pm. Quinn checked the window. It was dark and he could see the headlights of evening rush hour clearly below. There was a hum from the traffic but that was all.

At 5.50pm, Brady switched her phone on. At exactly 6pm it pinged.

It was Klein.

"HE'S ON THE MOVE."

Victoria Rogers' phone vibrated on the table.

"BE THERE SOON CAN'T WAIT."

"He's very old school," said Brady.

Klein texted again.

"WE'RE IN PICCADILLY."

Brady checked her gun,

"You ready for this Quinn?"

He nodded. The phone pinged again.

"NOW BOND STREET,"

Five minutes passed; the phone sounded again.

"HE'S OUTSIDE."

Jacob Candy got out of the back of his black Mercedes and punched the code to Rogers' building. Holding an expensive bunch of flowers, he bounded up the stairs like a man ready for a night of fun, but fun was not awaiting him. Both Quinn and Brady were on their feet standing.

Candy knocked on the door with the back of his hand. Quinn swung the door open, holding his gun with two hands at face height. Candy stared into the silencer; his breath taken away momentarily with the shock.

"We meet at last Jacob, or should I say Danny Boy."

Candy looked at him defiantly. He was a tall man, 52 years of age. Sandy coloured hair combed neatly to one side, blue pinstriped suit and handkerchief in his top breast pocket, complimented by an old regimental tie. He looked the archetypal Conservative M.P.

"Sorry, I don't believe we've met and where's Vicky?" (He said it was if he'd just arrived for afternoon tea).

"Don't worry about her, she's fine. You're right, we haven't met, but I'm sure you know who I am."

Candy shook his head slightly.

"Haven't got the foggiest old chap."

Brady stood in front of the large Adams fireplace that dominated the room, looking at the two men facing each other. She was puzzled for she had expected Candy to acknowledge Quinn, who gestured with his gun to Candy.

"Do sit down Jacob." Candy slowly entered the room, placing the flowers on a dark wooden D end table. Quinn closed the front door.

He sat down and looked at Brady. "And you are?"

"You should know who I fockin' am, as I've been doing some of your killing for you."

"Sorry, you've got me there. Do tell me what this is all about and perhaps we can clear things up."

Quinn sat on a chair opposite Candy. Now addressing Brady, he said,

"Meet the man who killed your father."

As Brady moved forward, she raised her gun. Candy held his hands up, in front of him, defensively.

"Woe, woe. I've never killed anyone in my life."

Brady looked doubtfully at Quinn.

"You're sure we've got the right man?"

Quinn placed his gun on the small wine table next to him. He leant forward with his elbows on his knees.

"Listen Candy, I know you're as guilty as hell, so put this lady out of her misery and tell her the truth."

Candy was very calm and cool. He looked over at Brady.

"Look, I'm terribly sorry, but I have nothing to tell, because I really don't know what you're talking about." He had a mannerism that was very convincing.

Brady leant down close to his face.

"Did you kill my Dah?"

Without warning, Candy jerked forward and head butted her, sending her crashing into the fireplace, her gun fell to the floor, Candy reached for it, but Quinn was quicker, grabbing his gun from the table, and fired just the once. Candy fell to his knees; the look of shock was etched on his face with the realisation that this was life's end. A red hole appeared where the bullet had entered just above his left eye. He stayed there on his knees, mouth wide open, frozen for maybe five seconds, he then slumped face down on the expensive wool carpet.

Brady pulled herself up. She had a cut across the bridge of her nose, they looked at each other. She picked up her gun.

Quinn checked Candy's body.

"He's dead alright."

Brady straightened her gun arm out.

"Stay still and don't get up. Slowly toss the gun to me."

"What is this about Helen?"

"Just do it." Her voice was stern and cold.

Quinn did as she asked.

"For all I know, you just killed the wrong man. I heard no confession, so the only way I can be sure I get the right man for my Dah, is to finish it like this."

Suddenly, the bedroom door opened, somehow Victoria Rogers, had wriggled free. Brady distracted, turned her head. Quinn quickly swung a small stool, hitting Brady. A shot fired missing Quinn with the bullet smashing into a family portrait. Quinn made for the door, as he opened it, a second shot smashed into the light switch next to him. He leapt down the stairs. Sparks flew off the metal banister next to him, as Brady fired down into the stairwell. Quinn pressed the green exit button by the front doors and ran out zig zagging through the rush hour traffic. Brady followed him down the stairs, just stopping short of the front glass doors. She composed herself and put her nuns head dress on, took off her gloves and then calmly made her way towards Green Park.

Quinn turned up Saville Row and then into Maddox Street. The night was cold with shoppers and commuters making their way down Regents Street. He was in a state of shock at what had just happened. A lot hinged on how many cameras if any, had picked them up, either on the way to, or from the killing. Would Rogers be able to ID him?

After a cab dropped him to his car, he sat in the driver's seat catching his breath. He reached into the glove box and took 40 mg of Escitalopram. God knows if it really helped. Maybe drugs were just a placebo. He decided to drive to his parents' home. He wanted to be there, if this was to be his last taste of freedom, it was with them he wanted to spend it.

As he drove home, the police were busy taking a statement, for they had already answered an emergency call from Victoria Rogers.

He arrived home just after 8.30pm. The light switched on in the hall, his mother opened the front door.

"We've been worried sick about you. She gave him another one of her strange hugs. "Now, come in and I'll do you something to eat."

On his way to the kitchen, he passed the lounge, where his dad had fallen asleep, with his glasses having slipped to the tip of his nose.

Quinn had to smile at the contrasting thoughts going through his head as his mother gossiped away to him about what the neighbours had been up to.

After he'd eaten only a small amount of what his mother had served up, he went inside, where his Dad was asleep, but snoring so loudly he woke himself up. As he peered over his glasses he said,

"Glad you're home son, you ok?"

"Not bad."

For two hours, the three of them watched Wycliffe on television, but Quinn just sat there, recounting events in his mind, checking his watch, thinking, *they would have found Candy by now, why aren't the police here?*

At 11pm Quinn heard the key in the door, it was Thomas, his brother, who stood just in the threshold of the lounge.

"Michael, where's the Bristol?"

"Still at Stansted, long story."

"You ok? Any news?"

Danny Boy

"All right if I tell you in the morning?"

He winked at his brother.

"No problem, I'm off to bed, as I'm knackered and have to be up at the crack of dawn."

Quinn's mother peered over the magazine she was reading.

"Let's have a tea, shall we?"

CHAPTER SIXTEEN

The Offertory, April 1999

It was early the next morning, when the house phone rang. Quinn was already awake having hardly slept, waiting for the police to arrive. He ran downstairs to the hallway to answer the phone.

"Hello Quinn, it's David Best."

Quinn sighed with relief.

"Sorry to ring you at your parents, but it was the last number I could try. I'd hoped you'd be there."

"That's ok."

"The reason I rang is that Jacob Candy has been found dead at a flat in Mayfair. A woman with him was tied to a bed but escaped, the police think it was a botched robbery."

"Oh, that's terrible David." Quinn tried his best to sound surprised.

The Offertory, April 1999

"Do the police have any ideas who killed him?"

"They raided a house in Abbey Wood and shot dead a woman in her mid-thirties. She was in possession of the gun they believe killed Candy. They are awaiting forensics. Any comment, I can put from an anonymous source?"

"Not from me David."

"Oh, and Quinn, your friend, Mark Taylor, gets buried today."

"That's quick, was the post-mortem done?"

"Done and dusted."

"One second, I have a note here. Ah yes, the funeral's at St Mary's Church in the village of Bibury, just outside Cirencester at 2.30pm."

"Thanks David,"

Quinn put the phone down. Were the authorities really not on to him? It seemed too good to be true. His brother came down the stairs.

"Everything ok Mike?"

"Yes, just about an old friend's funeral."

The two of them chatted and he told his brother that there was almost an inevitability that Brady's life would end like this. For her, she'd finally avenged her father's killing. It had been a long road, but for Quinn she had crossed the line where she seemed to relish taking other people's lives. He'd seen that himself in Ireland where some seemed to enjoy the act of killing. It went beyond the usual rules of engagement. She'd been quite an adversary. She'd tried to kill him and then saved him, then tried to kill him again. Klein was right, she was a nut job.

After his brother left, he got dressed and slid his original sim card back into his phone and left for the funeral. He arrived at Taylor's home little village just before the service started. The tranquillity of the area could not have been more of a contrast with the life Taylor had signed up for. Quinn parked his car outside St Mary's church which stands opposite a little primary school. It was typical funeral weather, cold and raining. Inside the church were only a handful of mourners. On top of the coffin was a picture of Taylor, showing him in his prime at 25 years of age in uniform, smiling at the camera. This would have been the around time Quinn had first met Taylor in Germany. His elderly parents sat at the front of the church. The eulogy by his eldest sister spoke of a shy young boy reluctantly going off to boarding school, which he hated and left at sixteen to go to the local grammar. He'd loved University and embraced his army career with enthusiasm until the tragedy of losing an eye and then even more tragically, his attempted suicide at his parent's home. She held back the tears until the very end. A military burial had been rejected, for Taylor's time in the army was not something that had happy memories for the family. In fact, it had destroyed him and them.

The mourners then followed the coffin to the cemetery, which was about 200 yards away, located next to the village hall. As his coffin was lowered into the grave, which already had started to fill with rainwater, the altar boys shivered as the vicar said a prayer under a large back umbrella. Two grave diggers stood a few yards back, drenched and waiting for the nod to infill the plot.

After speaking with Taylor's parents and politely turning down their invitation to come back to their house, he took the short walk to where his car was parked. Standing by the car was a figure of a tall man, his face was covered by the rim of his umbrella. As Quinn got nearer, he raised the umbrella.

"Afternoon Michael."

He recognised the waiting figure as Richard Lawson. He had a strange turtle like appearance, as for years he'd tried to make his 6ft 7" frame look shorter than it was, consciously trying to push his neck into his body which had left him with severely hunched shoulders. Since childhood he had been known as "Stretch." He had always been an outsider which made him perfect for intelligence work. It had been Lawson who'd arrived that night in the pub in Londonderry after the shooting. He'd quickly climbed the ranks and on leaving the army, had joined MI6.

Neither man attempted to shake hands as this was no social visit.

"Ah Quinn, awful business, like you, I knew Taylor in the North, lovely chap."

Quinn didn't reply. The rain started to get heavier. Lawson continued,

"Fancy a chat? Let's get out of the rain and go in. Heard the vicar say he was going back to the family home, so it should be empty."

They walked across the church grounds that were now deserted apart from two tourists taking pictures. The two men entered the church, which was adorned with various brass plaques, mainly dedicated to the fallen of the First World War.

The Offertory, April 1999

Lawson scanned the church.

"You know, you'd think there'd only been one fuckin' World War."

He looked at Quinn,

"Apart from funerals, I haven't been to church since I was a child, what about you Quinn?

"Still go occasionally."

"Must be the Catholic in you. Like a moth to a lightbulb." Lawson joked, but Quinn just looked ahead at the altar.

"I suppose you're wondering why I'm here?"

"I assume you're paying your respects like me."

"Not quite. Wanted to speak to you as we picked up your friend, Helen Brady last night at Heathrow."

Quinn hid his surprise that she was still alive. He sat down on a wooden pew.

Lawson stayed on his feet and looking down at Quinn said,

"You no doubt thought she was killed in the raid in Woolwich, but it was a woman, working with Brady who pulled a gun when our boys entered, shot on the spot. Brady won't talk to us, but Victoria Rogers has identified you both through photographs. We've got a gun and some gloves which no doubt will eventually lead back to you."

"So, you're the friendly face they've sent to bring me in?"

"Good God, no. Off the record, Quinn, there won't be too much mourning for that lunatic Candy. You see, he was supposed to be our new man for the future, but he got out of control. There is never a happy ending when the tail tries to wag the dog. We want to close this whole sorry business down, but we need some assurances from you. In simple terms Quinn, if you agree to go back to selling antiques or whatever it is you do and refuse to speak to the David Best's of this world, all this can go way, or you could find yourself, serving a long jail sentence with your Irish friend."

Quinn rotated a hymn book in his hands.

Lawson stared at Quinn who was sitting in silence.

Quinn sat back for a moment and looked up at Jesus on the cross. He then leant forward.

"Tell me Lawson, the shooting at Colonel Caine's place and Taylor's death, did you play a part?"

The Offertory, April 1999

Lawson thought for a moment before he answered.

"I believe it's time for honesty. Taylor was murdered on the orders of Candy, but when you were shot at Colonel Caine's, I won't lie to you Quinn, that was our boys. You see, Candy convinced counter terrorism that several ex- A14 officers were persons of interest. However, after Caine got shot, he mobilised friends in even higher places than Candy. It was the Colonel's intervention that changed things and Candy's timely death tidied things up nicely. The man had very quickly gone from rising star to becoming a liability."

"You mean I did your job for you?"

"Well sort of. Not sure we'd have bumped him off, though. His death can be played out as a bungled robbery. As far as Victoria Rogers is concerned, we could tell her the photographs she's identified are of people we do not know. I need to do a deal with you for your silence."

Quinn stood up,

"I need time to think about it."

Lawson leant across the bench he was sitting on and lit a cigarette off one of the church candles.

"You're not supposed to smoke in church."

"Don't tell anyone will you?" (The cheeky chappie act didn't work on Quinn).

Lawson stood up, his white socks clearly showing at the bottom of his quite not long enough trousers.

"Don't take too long making your mind up, will you, Quinn?"

"What will happen with Brady?"

Lawson pulled a face that only accentuated his horsey features.

"I'm sorry to say that anything she did up to last year, is basically pardoned by The Good Friday Agreement."

Lawson looked at his watch.

"She's due to take off from Heathrow in about an hour. The Irish police are waiting for her regarding the death of Shamus Kelly. They don't take kindly to one of their own being killed."

Quinn put the hymn book he'd been holding down.

The Offertory, April 1999

"Do you want to know what I think?"

"Try me."

"I think you're going to cover up the killings of Candy anyway."

Quinn got up and walked out of the church, leaving Lawson looking at the flickering candles.

CHAPTER SEVENTEEN

A very good Friday, October 1999

Six months later, on a Friday night, Quinn was making his way along Appleforth High Street. He was dressed in jeans and a shirt, flustered and late. As he entered the restaurant, his old friend Roberto greeted him.

"Where you fuckin' been Michael? You're keeping a lovely lady waiting. I've seated her by the window.

Quinn quickly made his way across the restaurant.

"I'm really sorry to keep you waiting. I've just opened my new shop and everything seemed to go wrong today."

"Don't worry, you're here now Michael."

Bruno the assistant manager came over and smiled.

"Ah good to see you Michael, can I get you both a drink?"

"Diet Coke," she said.

"And a Peroni for me."

A very good Friday, October 1999

He sat down.

His date looked beautiful, sitting there resting her chin on her hand. She was dressed simply in a powder blue trouser suit with a black silk blouse underneath. Her black hair fell over her shoulders. She drew admiring glance from other diners. Who was this new woman with Quinn?

Bruno brought the drinks to the table.

"Cheers said Quinn," and the clinked glasses with her.

"Well, I never imagined I'd be sitting opposite you on a date after all these years."

"When you asked for my number, I wasn't sure you'd call."

"Well, I've been thinking about asking you out since I was about twelve."

"Well after 32 years, your patience has paid off!" She laughed.

"Do your parents know you're here?"

"No, I had to tell a big white lie and said I was going back up north overnight to stay with a friend."

They chatted with ease, for they had a shared history in many ways. After the meal and some ribbing from Roberto, they walked along the high street towards Quinn's flat, which was above his newly opened shop.

As they reached her car, parked nearby, he turned to her,

"Priya, as your parents think you're away overnight, do you want to stay at my place."

She turned and put her hands on each of his shoulders.

Michael, I'm shocked you would say such a thing. What sort of girl do you think I am? I've already booked a room in a pub."

He looked embarrassed and apologetically said,

"I meant; I can sleep on the couch."

She laughed.

"Michael, you're not very good at this are you? Of course, I'd like to stay."

She kissed him on the mouth. It was long and it was passionate, and he was taken aback.

He smiled. "Just one thing, promise me there will be no surprises!"

"What do you mean?"

A very good Friday, October 1999

"Oh, nothing really, it's just last time I tried to spend the night with someone, I nearly ended up dead."

"Well, hopefully, this time you'll merely be dead impressed!"

The next morning, as the sun broke through the shuttered windows, Quinn awoke and smiled, he certainly was *dead impressed*. Her closed eyes accentuated her long eye lashes. In the early morning light, she looked more beautiful now, than when he'd known her as a teenager. She opened her eyes and caught him smiling.

"What's so funny?"

"I was just thinking. All those years ago when were kids playing in the garden, I would never have imagined, we'd end up like this. You here, lying beside me."

She laughed again. *It was a laugh he'd like to get used to.*

"After last night, I might go veggie myself," laughed Quinn.

Quinn got out of bed.

"Tea or coffee?"

"Tea of course! Don't forget, no milk."

Quinn made two teas and handed one to Priya as she sat up in bed placing a pillow behind her back. He slipped on some jeans and a tee shirt. "I'm just popping down to the Post Office to pick up a record I've ordered for a customer. He almost skipped along the street. The last few months he had settled firmly back into the quiet life he wanted. Would it last? Would he and Priya have a future? Who knows? However, there was an uncomfortable feeling he felt every morning when he got up and then it would pass, but every morning it was there.

In his eye line on the other side of the narrow High Road, was a familiar figure sitting on a green wooden bench, it was Lawson. He was wearing check trousers, and a windbreaker, looking very much the regular weekend golfer. Quinn slowly crossed the road.

"You following me Lawson?"

"More watching over you really?"

"I get the feeling you don't trust me"

"Don't be silly, I had hoped I'd have heard from you by now."

"I think I've already proved to you that I'm not rushing off to speak to anyone."

"A nice signed document, would make me feel much better."

A very good Friday, October 1999

"We'll see, "said Quinn.

Lawson yawned and leant back, outstretching his long legs and looking up at Quinn said,

"Believe it or not, we are worried about you. We think you're in danger from Brady. Sad to say, she did a deal with our colleagues in Dublin. Gave a few names which rather surprised us, but I suspect she has one thing on her mind above any loyalty she may have felt to her old friends, *you!*" She's moved north of the border in a place called Cushendall and shacked up with an ex-bomber called Connor Sheehan, they make a lovely couple."

"What makes you think Brady is after me?"

Lawson leant forward.

"Sheehan has a lady friend who's an informer. He let it slip to her, that Brady and him are planning to kill a certain ex-army captain in the next few months. Who can they be thinking of Michael? How many ex- army captains can there be, that she hates enough to target? Now, we can tail them if they enter the mainland but if they give us the slip, they could turn up anywhere. It could be here with your lovely new girlfriend, (very nice, by the way), or at your parent's house. Unfortunately, we can't go around taking out terrorist like the good old days. There'd be a major shit storm, but if we were to find someone who could slip in and out of Ireland quietly, preferably not a member of the security forces, it would solve the problem for both of us."

"If Brady is coming for me, it would certainly solve a problem for you."

"Quinn you're such a cynic. We don't need any more mysterious deaths, thank you. At least take my card and think about it. We both might sleep better at night."

The second Quinn reached out to take that card, they both knew he had his man.

CHAPTER EIGHTEEN
374 Yards, November 1999

Two weeks later, Quinn arrived from London Euston at Liverpool Lime Street Station. He'd shared his carriage with a rabble of West Ham away fans, so was relieved when the train pulled into the station. Two hours of having, "I'm forever blowing bubbles," sung to him and how they "All hate Tottenham." It was more than he could handle. The train journey was just over two hours. Waiting at the top of the platform was a young army driver. She was holding a sign up, reading: MR QUINN. She drew admiring looks and many unwanted comments as the fans filed passed her. Quinn walked up to her,

"Well, the army's improved since my day."

There were no smiles no reaction, just an outstretched arm for a handshake and a "I'm Corporal Lewis, follow me sir."

They went outside and down the concrete steps that stretch out in front of the station. Parked diagonally across the road was a black Lotus Carlton with a driver at the wheel of the high-powered saloon. The corporal opened the boot of the car and Quinn put his bag into it. He got in the back; the girl got into the front next to the driver. They roared passed the Adelphi and drove along Renshaw Street at high speed. He attempted conversation in the car, but all three occupants soon fell into silence. The car arrived after around twenty minutes at the picturesque Sunlight Village. Created during Victorian times for its workers, the village is an oasis in what was an industrial landscape but what had now become an industrial wasteland. The car stopped outside a large house opposite a bowling green. He followed the corporal up to the front door, the car pulled away.

She took him into the house and into an area that was a large operations room. Sitting at a boardroom sized table was a sergeant of around forty years of age.

"This is Sergeant Hay. He will talk you through the operation."

Thank you. That will be all," said the sergeant.

She then left the room.

"This way sir," said Hay, who was tall, maybe six feet, two, and looked slightly oriental, *mother or father must've been Chinese or Japanese*, Quinn thought. His voice was quite clipped, but not too posh, *possibly grammar school*. He had

374 Yards, November 1999

an almost school master manner about him as he explained the plan.

On one of the walls were various photographs and ordnance surveys pinned to it. He began.

"This is a picture of Brady's house where she lives with a chap called Connor Sheehan."

He pointed to an aerial picture of a white farmhouse with a rusty tin roofed barn next to it. He then drew Quinn's attention to a map with a red line drawn across it with a measurement written in red next to it.

"It's 374 yards from this vantage point to the front door. We will supply you with the weapon you've requested which will be hidden in a compartment under the rear seat of a Londonderry registered Land Rover Discovery. At 10.30 tomorrow night, you will drive onto the ferry to Belfast and then drive to Cushendall, you should get there for around 8am. There's a house near the village, the address of which you will need to memorise. There you will meet Jimmy Burn, he's a local who's been working for us for years. He will take you to a field next to Brady's house, you may have to wait hours, maybe a day, until she appears. Once done, drop the gun back to Burns. We've booked you on the last ferry back the night after tomorrow. You will leave the car you arrived in at Jimmy's and take a UK registered vehicle, we've organised, back. If you call us on your arrival in Liverpool, we will meet you here for a debrief and organise getting you back to London.

"Any questions?"

Quinn shook his head.

"So, Captain Quinn, practice is tomorrow at 8.30am."

After a sleepless night, Quinn was picked up at 8am, and taken to the Forestry firing range ten miles outside Liverpool. Quinn went inside and standing at the reception was Sergeant Dennis McKay. Five foot six, stocky with a large round baby face, with short brill creamed hair flattened across the top of his head.

"Nice to meet you capin'," he said in a broad Glaswegian accent.

"Please follow me."

He led Quinn to the front of a booth on the firing range. On the bench was a weapon Quinn knew well. He'd supplied enough in his time to know the gun inside out. McKay picked it up and stood the weapon on its end.

374 Yards, November 1999

"I'm sure you recognise the Barret M82A 1277mm automatic rifle, along with the Armalite, an IRA favourite. Accurate range of over a mile. No current body armour can provide protection against it. Quinn had asked for this gun, as the killing would have the look of a Republican squabble rather than a British planned assassination. He felt the guns weight and nestled the stock into his shoulder. He looked through the telescopic sights.

"It's loaded capin', would you like to give it a try?"

The targets were metal outlines of soldiers running towards you. Attached just over the heart area were targets, like you would see on a dartboard. The first shot didn't even hit, the second struck the metal shoulder. Quinn turned his head away from the sites for a moment and refocussed. Then three shots rang out.

"Good shootin' capin, one bollseye and two fractionally below," said McKay.

Quinn practiced for the next four hours, hitting the different targets from different angles, until he felt confident with the weapon.

Just before 2pm, Lawson arrived.

"Afternoon Quinn, I hear McKay is very impressed with your shooting. Should come as no surprise though."

Quinn gave a modest shrug. Lawson took off the thin leather gloves he was wearing, he leant back against the wall with his arms folded, watching Quinn hit the target again and again.

"Well, I'd say you're ready, wouldn't you Quinn?"

Quinn said nothing, but he knew the only way he'd have closure was to stop Brady. Lawson finished a phone call and turned to Quinn.

"The car will bring you back at 4pm Quinn, I suggest you get fed and showered and rested before you leave.

Outside McKay put the rifle into Quinn's car, Lawson leaned his tall frame towards Quinn and in almost a whisper said,

"By the way Quinn, there will be 50K put into your account as a little thankyou from Her Majesty."

Quinn said nothing as this was not about money, but he certainly wasn't going to refuse it.

CHAPTER NINETEEN

It's been fun. October 1999

That evening as Quinn arrived on the outskirts of Liverpool, he remembered when he'd first come to Liverpool in 1975 seeing kids in their bare feet climbing through a hoarding. It was the first time he'd seen such poverty. It was like a scene from a 1930's Pathe news reel. The later 1980's development and preservation of the Albert Docks had been a game changer for the city.

As he drove through Birkenhead, he passed the derelict buildings of businesses long gone. At the terminal, a border guard checked his ticket and waved him into a queue on the dockside. As he looked across the Mersea, he could see The Liver Building, the Anglican Cathedral and the St John's Beacon tower blinking in the distance.

The cars started to move onto the boat. After two hours in the bar he went to his cabin, which was more comfortable than he'd expected. He lay in the bunk and tried to sleep but couldn't. At 5.45am. a tannoy in the room sounded that they would dock at 6.30am and passengers were expected to vacate their cabins by 6am.

Quinn got ready and went upstairs and bought a coffee. At 6.50am he pulled onto the M2 out of the Belfast Dock area and then the A8 to Larne. He'd decided to take the coast road to Cushendall to avoid any possibility of being stopped. The sea and coastline looked beautiful, revealing the beauty of the island, taking you through Milltown, Glenarm and Glenariff. The views of the rolling hills and the glens are quite spectacular. The lack of investment in the area, because of the troubles has left Northern Ireland unspoilt in so many ways. *This*, thought Quinn, *is the real Ireland.* He'd been through Cushendall before as he'd regularly meet in the nearby Ballycastle, which is a pretty town with a picturesque beach and a golf course. Not the sort of place you would have thought Loyalists would target to bomb the Catholic church or the IRA to attack the Marine Hotel, which it bombed in 1979.

As he drove along the narrow roads, it wasn't hard to spot the Protestant villages, for they displayed Union Jack's on flagpoles in front gardens with pride. A thick mist descended off the sea. It slowed him down, so it took just over an hour and a half to get to his destination. Quinn pulled into the yard of the address he'd been given. The place looked neglected. Jimmy Burn appeared in the doorway. He was stick thin, around seventy years of age, so older than Quinn had expected. His clothing hung loose

It's been fun. October 1999

on him. He had a mop of grey unkept hair. He watched Quinn park the mud spattered Land Rover next to his old Fiat. He called out to him.

"Morning, I recognise you from the photographs. Come in."

He moved away from the doorway and went back into the house. Quinn ran quickly through the rain that had started to fall heavily.

He followed Burn into the kitchen.

"Tea?"

"Yes, just black, please," said Quinn.

"Just boiled the kettle, good Irish weather, isn't it?"

Burn had an educated Northern Irish accent, which almost eradicates the Irish pronunciation.

"Been in Ireland a long time?" asked Quinn.

He turned from the tea he was pouring.

"Answer no questions, tell no lies. Probably less you know about me the better."

Quinn felt he'd just been put in his place. Burn placed a tea in front of Quinn.

"Right then, to business."

He placed a photograph on the table, it was the same picture Quinn had seen two nights before.

"I'm going take you here, (he pointed to the aerial photograph), where you will have clear sight of the target."

As Quinn looked closer at the picture, Burn placed a small canvas bag on one of the kitchen chairs.

"There's food and drink in there to keep you going."

Quinn got back into his Land Rover and followed Burn's old 4 x 4 Fiat Panda for around ten minutes. They passed an old sign for Cushendall and then turned left into a muddy field. The Discovery struggled on the thick mud. They pulled up at the edge of a field by a hawthorn hedge. They got out and Burn's handed Quinn some field binoculars. The rain was pouring.

"Down there, see it?"

Through the lenses, he could see the house. There was no sign of activity. In the yard was an old tractor and some ancient farming equipment. The open sided barn next to the house was empty.

Burn pulled up his collar.

It's been fun. October 1999

Well, best I leave you to it, you know where I am. I will see you when you come back to switch cars. Just leave everything in the Discovery for me. The keys for the return car, which will be a red Cavalier, will be on the sun visor."

He didn't shake Quinn's hand or wish him luck. He just got back in his car, which slid around as he looped the field and he then left through the opened gate.

Quinn opened the side door of the Land Rover and lifted up the seat. With a screwdriver he prized open the hidden compartment and retrieved the Barrat M8. He loaded it, attached the sights and focused on the front door of the house. This, he thought, is where he'd take out Brady and if need be, her boyfriend, the bomber. Quinn checked his watch. It was 10.15am. Dusk would be around 4.30pm. He had night sights, but a daytime shot would be preferable.

He took out a ground sheet and lay it over a shallow ditch and positioned himself on his front, raising the binoculars. Another seven long hours passed, when an orange Austin Allegro drew up in front of the house. A male of around forty years of age got out, Quinn put his eye to the sights of the gun. He could see it was Sheehan, who'd opened the front door but had left it open. He appeared to be calling to someone. *This has to be Brady*, thought Quinn. The sight was focussed on the open doorway. His finger twitched slightly as it touched the trigger. He could feel his pulse throbbing. He was ready, he was set, when suddenly a voice from behind him said,

"Don't fockin' move Quinn."

It was like history repeating itself, he recognised the voice, for it was Brady. He stayed perfectly still. He turned his head away from the sights and lay there frozen.

"Throw the gun forward and slowly get to your knees and keep your hands high".

With a push, the gun slid down the bank in front of him. He got onto his knees. The wet mud pressed through his combat trousers.

"Now sit on your hands, cross legged."

He shuffled round, doing as he was told. He felt vulnerable and stupid.

He looked at her standing there, confident and defiant. As usual, in black, she was holding a sawn-off light weight shotgun in her hands. Her hair blew in the wind which reddened her cheeks.

"How did you know Helen?"

It's been fun. October 1999

"Lawson. I was stopped at Heathrow the day after we got Candy. They flew me to Belfast, keeping me well away from Dublin's jurisdiction. After two days in custody, Lawson arrived. He said that your silence couldn't be guaranteed, so if I was prepared to kill you, not only would I have immunity from prosecution on both sides of the border, but the only other person who could implicate me in Candy's killing would be gone, namely you. As a bonus, I'd be killing the man involved in my father's death.

Now the thing is, the moment that bastard offered me the deal, I knew what you had told me about what happened in my dah's house must've been true. If he doesn't trust you to keep quiet, it doesn't make sense that you were part of my dah's killing.

She lowered the gun, pointing it at the ground.

"Humour me, Helen, what was to happen next?"

"The arrangement was, he'd get you here and if I failed to kill you, yah man Burn, would finish you off when you go back to the house to switch cars. Lawson must be a naïve bastard if he thinks I'd do his bidding for him."

"What now?"

She shrugged,

I'm outta here. Lawson's immunity deal has given me a way out. I'm fockin' exhausted with all this shite anyway. Every focker I meet turns out to be a liar."

She flipped the gun up and rested it over her shoulder.

"Stay safe Quinn, sorry about what happened in London, it's been fun."

And with that simple remark, she turned and trudged across the heavy mud and was gone.

Quinn stood for a moment in disbelief.

Fucking fun! Is she serious?

He got into the Land Rover and was just about to turn the key and stopped. He thought, *there must be a tracker, but where?* He picked up the ground sheet he'd been lying on, grabbed a torch from the storage box at the back, and a wheel brace that was flattened at one end. He slid under and shone a light along the rear of the car. There was no sign of anything. He got up and slid the ground sheet under the front of the car. Again, he shone a light. At first, he couldn't see nothing, then there it was, bolted to the underside of the vehicle, with a wire leading to it. Quinn knew it would have a battery that acts as a backup, so it would keep sending a signal, maybe for a couple of days.

It's been fun. October 1999

As long as it stayed in one place, pulsing out a signal, Lawson's men would think he was still there until Burn checked on him. He used the brace as a crowbar and levered into a gap between the tracker and the underside of the Land Rover's floor. There was a clang as bolts snapped and the tracker fell away. Quinn picked it up and scrambled to his feet. He placed it by the ditch running alongside the field. He threw the mobile phone Lawson's team had given him as that would be monitored also. *How long would he have before they knew he was gone?* Maybe twelve hours.

He started the Land Rover up and pulled onto the main road and headed for the A2 leading to Belfast. From a call box he rang Stenna and all they could offer him was a Three hour crossing into Cairnryan in Scotland. Using his credit card, he booked a crossing, (would he get flagged up)? It was dark, and he'd be unlucky to be caught. The journey took just over an hour. This old city to him, was the one place that represented all that was wrong with Northern Ireland, he didn't like it at all.

He arrived at the docks just in time and quoted his booking number. *Is this where someone would come out of the woodwork and stop him?*

"Lane four, enjoy your journey, "said a smiling face. It was 10pm.

The cars started to move; he parked the Land Rover on board. He bought a tea and a sandwich and sat amongst families with young children. As he finished his tea, an announcement came over the tannoy to say the ship would dock 15 minutes late due to the fog. Quinn closed his eyes but his brain was on high alert, how could it not be? Here he was, on the Irish Sea, a target for the very service he had served with such loyalty. How could he secure his own safety? He needed something on Lawson who would be a hard man to catch out, but there must be something. He knew Lawson was a loner and in Quinn's experience, loners have a naivety when it comes to sex and that made them vulnerable. This Quinn decided, would be the way to get to him.

The sea was calm, which was of great relief to Quinn. He went outside on the blue painted deck for a cigarette but cursed himself for starting again. The ships horn sounded several times as it cut its way through the fog. The deck was deserted, it was cold and raining, the wind was just getting up. A young man came out with an unlit cigarette in his mouth. He approached Quinn.

"Would you have a wee light?"

"Sure". Quinn handed him his lighter.

It's been fun. October 1999

Quinn warily watched him light the cigarette. In the wind it glowed brightly. *This would be the perfect place to bump me off and lose me at sea,* thought Quinn.

"Thanks a million," said the young man, who handed the lighter back and carried on walking. Quinn sighed with relief. Every stranger seemed a danger to him.

I'm getting paranoid, he thought.

He went back inside to his seat, but there was now an old guy asleep across two chairs including Quinn's. He grabbed a place at the bar and ordered a lager.

An hour passed and drivers were instructed to return to their cars. Quinn sat in his car anxiously awaiting the ramp to lower. When it did, he could see the outline of the Cairnryan hills through the darkness. As he drove out there were two police officers in the middle of the road just in front of the border control office. *Would this be it?* But no, they just waved him through. The journey to London was long and tiring with miles of unlit roads. Passing places such as Lockerbie and Gretna on the A75 and then after two and a half hours moving onto the M6 where you almost immediately see the sign "Welcome to Cumbria, England." Quinn pushed the car up to eighty miles per hour. The diesel engine rattled away happily. He passed through the Lake District, The Dales, The Peak District, he passed Sheffield and Northampton, arriving in London at just before 8am.

He parked the car near Finsbury Park underground station and caught the train to South Kensington. Quinn checked back into The Ramada Hotel and that evening as he sat in the bar, he spotted the prostitute who he'd spoken to in the bar the previous month. As he approached her, she smiled recognising him.

"You look better than when I last saw you."

"Thanks love, I was wondering if you and a friend would like to earn two grand…"

CHAPTER TWENTY

Fore! November 2000

It was a cold Sunday morning as Quinn approached one of the security barriers to St Georges Estate, Surrey, home to the famous St George's Hill Golf Club, one of the oldest and most prestigious clubs in England. Surrounded by a private estate of large houses, all of which have extensive grounds. A security guard came to the window of the old Bristol motor car that Quinn had finally got back from Stansted. For once it fitted in perfectly with the surroundings.

"Morning, I'm meeting Richard Lawson for breakfast,"

The guard seemed distracted at the sight of Quinn's car, to the point where he didn't check any notes or messages regarding any visitors for Richard Lawson.

"No problem, sir." And he raised the barrier, admiring the vehicle as it glided by.

Quinn drove along the approach roads, passing mansion after mansion, many owned by new Russian investors, who hardly ever use them. From the car park, Quinn made his way up the slope and then pass the pro shop turning left into the club house. He entered through two open large oak doors. The hallway at St George's is like the entrance to a country house. The interior walls are wooden panelled, displaying names and photographs of former winners and captains. He climbed the stairs and in the first room on the right was a small group of players having breakfast, past which, Quinn could see Richard Lawson sat at a table on his own, by a window overlooking the ninth hole. He was a low handicap golfer, that belied his gangly physique.

He was quite a fixture at the club on a Sunday. He'd ordered his usual, scrambled eggs with black coffee and had started to read the Sunday Telegraph. He looked up and recognised the figure walking towards him. Quinn sat down.

"Who let you in?" said Lawson.

He looked at Quinn as if there was a nasty smell in the room.

"I think getting into your golf club, wasn't my biggest all-time challenge. I must say, it's very nice, never played here myself."

Lawson seemed lost for words.

Quinn passed an envelope over the table.

Fore! November 2000

"What's this?" Said Lawson.

"Something I prepared earlier."

Lawson opened the envelope and looking at the pictures and then looking at Quinn exclaimed,

"Jesus Christ!"

He quickly shoved the pictures back into the envelope.

Quinn sat back. A waiter came along.

"Is sir eating?"

"Ah, yes please. I'll have two brown toast and a black tea for me, no milk, thank you."

Once the waiter moved away, Quinn continued.

"You should be more careful how you spend your evenings. I particularly like the one of you with just your socks on, with two young girls in a hotel room. Dear me, and you're married to who is it, Colonel Jackson's Daughter? What will he say? There's even one of them opening your briefcase with secret documents in it, while you're blindfolded handcuffed to a bed."

"You fucking bastard."

A few heads turned towards them.

"Happy to say, a live fucking bastard, no thanks to you."

The tea and toast arrived.

"As a bonus, I do have a nice video to go with the pictures."

"How will sir be paying?"

"Mr Lawson."

Lawson gave a begrudging nod to the waiter. He looked as if he could explode, but he knew he was cornered.

Quinn sipped tea from a small china cup. He leant forward spreading the marmalade onto the toast and spoke,

"Now I'm not one to hold a grudge, but let's be honest for once. For years you've been tipping the wink at some very nasty men. Making out to be one thing, when you're really another. You set me up to be killed, you failed, so it's pay up time."

"What do you want?"

"You make sure I stay safe and none of your bedroom athletics needs to come out.

There was no reply, Lawson just sat in stony silence.

Quinn finished his drink.

"Oh, don't forget the fifty grand you promised to put in my account!"

He stood up.

"One thing that surprised me Stretch, was you falling for the oldest trick in the book."

Lawson just sat, as if in a trance.

Quinn left and as he got into his car, he smiled, as for the first time, he finally felt in control.

CHAPTER TWENTY-ONE

Two of Us

Two hours later, Quinn stopped outside a neat, terraced house in Ilford. He'd rehearsed what he was going to say. (It had been four weeks since he and Priya had spent the night together). He'd told her he'd had to go to Ireland to help an old friend out, which was sort of true!

Right, he thought.

He walked up the path, he was nervous. He rang on the doorbell and stood back. After about a minute, Priya opened the door. She was wearing traditional Indian clothing. She leant on the door frame and folded her arms.

Quinn stood back defensively and only half-jokingly asked,

"You found a single vegetarian nondrinking professional Hindu man to marry yet?"

"Still looking," she smiled.

"How was Ireland?"

Two of Us

"All sorted, I hope."

"I came with a proposal."

"Well, what's your proposal?"

"Would you like to marry a meat eating, non-professional, non- Hindu alcoholic?"

She looked shocked but couldn't help smile, and was trying to process what Quinn had just said, and so was he!

"I'm afraid my parents won't be happy with such a proposal."

"I'm not looking to marry your parents!"

He moved forward and she held her hand up.

"You better come in and speak to my Dad."

Quinn felt a bit child-like as if he had been summoned to meet the grown ups. He wasn't sure Priya actually wanted to marry him, but as he had just blurted his proposal out, he was going to run with it. He followed her into the hallway, the walls of which were decorated with a mix of family photographs and religious pictures. There was a sweet smell of cooking. He didn't know what it was, but it reminded him of when they were small children and they would both sit on the back doorstep of her parent's old house, eating something out of a bowl he couldn't pronounce.

Priya lead him into a rear lounge where her Mum and Dad were seated on separate armchairs. The room was decorated in garish colours that clashed badly. On the walls were more family photographs and on shelves were an odd assortment of ornaments dedicated to the Hindu religion. Priya's father had like Quinn's Dad been at Fords all his working life, while his wife stayed at home, raising five children of which, Priya was the oldest. To Quinn, this felt far worse than any meeting he'd ever had with the army top brass, or any terrorist group come to that.

Priya tried her best to be very casual about Quinn's arrival.

"Look who's come to see us?"

Both parents looked up from the television.

"Hello Michael, How's your Mum and dad?"

"Good, thank you."

"You're both looking well," he said, trying a bit of false flattery.

There was an uncomfortable silence, then Priya's mum said,

"Priya's just made some tea for us all Michael, do join us."

Priya went to the kitchen and Quinn sat at one end of a sofa, as far away from her parents as possible.

Her Mum spoke first.

"Priya told us, she'd seen you at the Shannon Club some months back. We don't like her working there. All that drinking and who knows what?"

At this point her father didn't speak, for he was no stranger to drink, but inside the home, he was a strict non-drinking Hindu. Quinn continued,

"Yes, we bumped into each other, I was with my brother, Tom."

"Ah yes, the teacher, that's right, yes?

"Yes, that's our Tom alright."

Another silence followed.

Priya's father was suspicious. In a stern tone he said,

"So, what brings you to our home, certainly not to see two old people like us?"

"It's Priya I came to see, but it's good to see you looking so well." The flattery overload continued!

"And why would you visit a married Hindu woman?"

His manner had turned quite aggressive.

Priya entered the room with a tray of tea and cake and tried to change the subject.

"Isn't it great to see Michael after all these years?"

As she crouched forward to hand her father some tea, he leant to one side, so he could see around her.

"Why would you call to see my married daughter?"

"Dad, Michael and me have known each other since we were small, we're just old friends."

Priya had lost courage when confronted by her father. Her mother glared at Quinn, she had a feeling there was more to this story. Quinn cut to the chase.

"Look, I'd like to marry your daughter once her divorce is through."

Nobody said a word, her parents looked at each other and then at Priya, who was now sitting on the same settee as Quinn, with her head bowed looking at the floor. The tension in the room was palpable.

First her father spoke.

"Is this true, you want to marry this man, this…, this soldier?" He couldn't have said it in a more derogatory way even if he tried.

"Ex-soldier, if you don't mind," said Quinn, trying to lighten the mood.

Priya sat there in silence with tears running down her cheeks. It was an awkward scene, especially as Priya wasn't saying no or yes to Quinn's bad timed proposal.

Priya's father looked at her.

"Well child, is this what you want?"

"Dad, I'm not a child but when I was, you arranged for me to marry someone which I went ahead with, to please you and Mum, and apart from my two boys, all it brought me was unhappiness. I want to be happy now. Do you want me to be alone for the rest of my life?"

Tears continued to flow down her face.

Her Dad looked at her Mum and then back at Priya and shrugging his shoulders said,

"We cannot accept this man as your husband. Do you want to bring shame onto your family?"

Her mother interrupted.

"Priya, you must obey your father, Michael, you should leave."

Quinn stood up to go, he felt deflated and defeated.

To his utter shock Priya said,

"Michael, I'm coming with you."

Her father shouted, "If you leave with him, you're no longer our daughter."

She stood her ground and looked at Quinn. He could see, she was determined.

"Ok, Michael let's go."

Quinn followed her out to his car, no knowing what to say. They sat inside the car for a moment, and he turned to her and said,

"Are you sure this is what you want?"

"I've been trying to please them all my life Michael, not anymore. I'm forty-four and they talk to me like I'm a little kid. *Priya do this, Priya do that.*"

"You're really as old as that?"

"Start the bloody car, Michael."

As he turned the key, he looked towards Priya's house, and he could see her mother standing and wiping her eyes in the doorway. He couldn't help feeling bad, but what could he do or say?

And In The End

Five months later, Quinn woke up by the side of his new wife who was still asleep. Thankfully her mother was talking to her by phone occasionally, but her dad still wasn't. Priya had told Quinn that her mum had come round to the idea of them being married, but she was yet to win her Dad over. Her parents had boycotted the wedding, but her sisters had attended, which made it a lovely day, starting at a registry office and then a reception at Roberto's.

As Quinn got up, there was a clunk as the newspaper dropped through the letter box. He went down the stairs of the cottage he'd only recently bought and picked up the paper. The image that jumped out from the front of the paper, shocked him. It was a picture of Richard Lawson, with the story of a British Civil servant, who'd fallen under a train at Paddington Station. The police were looking for a nun who might have witnessed the incident.

Well, well, thought Quinn. *Brady obviously had decided not to go as quietly as she claimed.* He knew his insurance policy had just disappeared on the railway tracks, but so too had his nemesis who he hadn't trusted to keep to keep his side of the bargain anyway. He hadn't heard from Lawson ever again, after that morning at St Georges. (but at least he had received the 50K).

As for Lawson's successor, he would know of Quinn, but it wouldn't be personal. He was determined to just take one day at a time. Maybe this would be as near as he'd get to a happy ending.

The End

Printed in Great Britain
by Amazon